BOOKS BY

MONROE ENGEL

NOVELS

STATUTES OF LIMITATIONS   1988

FISH   1981

VOYAGER BELSKY   1962

THE VISIONS OF NICHOLAS SOLON   1959

A LENGTH OF ROPE   1952

CRITICISM

THE USES OF LITERATURE *(editor)*   1973

THE MATURITY OF DICKENS   1959

STATUTES
OF
LIMITATIONS

MONROE ENGEL

STATUTES
OF
LIMITATIONS

ALFRED A. KNOPF

NEW YORK

1988

THIS IS A BORZOI BOOK
PUBLISHED BY ALFRED A. KNOPF, INC.

Copyright © 1988 by Monroe Engel

Library of Congress Cataloging-in-Publication Data

Engel, Monroe.
    Statutes of Limitations.

    I. Title.
PS3555.N388S74   1988   813'.54   87-46078
ISBN 0-394-57040-5

Manufactured in the United States of America
First Edition

STATUTES
OF
LIMITATIONS

I

THE SOMEWHAT VEILED look of that portion of his daughter's face Ben Morrison could see as she embraced her mother, and the way her one visible eye searched his face, suggested at once that he and Lucky hadn't come home to simple continuity. Something must have occurred in their absence that they'd now have to reckon with, and this didn't entirely surprise him. He'd had a gloomy premonition that their absence would not be uneventful, that either Faith would be worse before they got back or that Sarah and Carl would have another falling out. And since he knew already that there had been no significant change in Faith's health—he'd heard Sarah say as she and Lucky threw their arms around each other, "She's been okay, not great but okay"—he was pretty sure of the general character at least of what had gone wrong. There was likely to be a lot of silent inquiry though before he'd know just what it was.

Ocular research was their family habit. There were only three people with whom he'd had regular exchange since he'd sold his business—his wife Lucky, his daughter Sarah, and his mother-in-law Faith—and of the three, only Faith practiced freedom of speech very regularly. In her case moreover, this reflected a kind of disinterestedness that created its own limitations. She was now approaching her eighty-fifth birthday, and though her engagement with existence was still keen, it had narrowed a lot in the past few years. He could count on her to say what she thought however and to ask for what few things she still wanted, whereas with Lucky particularly, but with Sarah sometimes too, he had to be on the alert for readable signs. And Sarah and Lucky in turn had similar difficulties with him. They were all candid enough in what they did say to each other, but their candor could also be a form of camouflage, something offered to cover what was being withheld. They lived together consequently in an affectionate peace that was often remarkably arduous.

He'd actually been practicing this uncertain form of inquiry off and on for a while already. When the garrulous pilot came on the p.a. for the fifth or sixth time since they'd left Mexico City to let them know that they were passing over Baltimore and would be landing in Boston in fifty-two minutes, he'd been assaulted by a familiar diffuse unease. For ten days now, on vacation, he'd done nothing and tried to enjoy it. But what made this vacation distinctive was that he didn't know very well what he'd be doing when he got back either. As for the past three months, there'd be so little he had to do for some time to come still that only initiative could keep him out of the ranks of the idle. And when he looked at Lucky to see how she responded to the pilot's announcement, what he saw first was that he must already be wearing the brand of idleness. He'd meant to ask her whether she thought there'd be anyone at the airport to meet them, but at that moment the plane banked, and in the consequent rush of pale light through the window next to her, her face was so arrestingly florid that he said nothing. He was thinking instead that this was going to be an unseasonable color when they got home. Out below them now the ground was pale as the light, sere faded fields mottled with snow.

The arrested question though would have been more particular than it pretended. Since neither of their sons lived anywhere near Boston any longer—Mark was in Duluth and Phil in Los Angeles—only Sarah could meet them. He knew how hard it was for her to leave work in the middle of the afternoon though, so that if she was at Logan when they arrived he'd wonder what mixture of affection and some other urgency had brought her there. He'd be watching for the familiar twist in the left corner of her mouth, that nervous meeting of her thin expressive lips that he knew as a sign that something was amiss.

Lucky had been too intent on the book she'd been reading even to notice when he turned toward her across the empty seat between them, and he abandoned his question, unbuckled his seat belt, and walked to the lavatories in the rear of the plane. Inside one of the cubicles, his knees braced against the bowl, he could see how much sunshine he too had absorbed in the time they'd been away. Something less though than Lucky's high radiance was reflected in the flattening, fluorescent sheen of the glass. His sexagenarian's skin tanned only to a leathery brown now that he didn't admire even in August when it was relatively inconspicuous, but that looked flagrantly unappealing in March. The same drab color on the backs of his hands which he could see directly, without the intervention of the mirror, also accentuated the fine lines in the slackened skin.

As he returned to his seat then, he observed that everyone on the plane except the flight attendants and the Mexican passengers was marked by this same unseasonable stain. Worst though were the Acapulco group occupying a block of seats in the broad center section. They'd boarded together each wearing a sombrero with Montezuma Tours stamped across the crown, and they'd all shown symptoms of extreme sleep deprivation as well as of dangerous over-exposure to the sun. Half or more of them were wearing their sombreros right now, slanted down over their eyes to encourage sleep but maybe also to dull the ardor of their skin. Except for the Mexican passengers however, only the flight attendants—and not just the gringos, but the two black stewardesses and the Puerto Rican steward who was the chief Spanish speaker—had any winter pallor.

When he sat down again, Lucky closed her book, stretched, and asked if he knew where they were. "You didn't hear our talkative friend in the cockpit orienting us again a few minutes ago?" He asked the question with a mixture of admiration and skepticism.

"Would I have asked where we were if I had?"

"I suppose not," he said. "Anyway, we were just clearing Baltimore, which means we ought to be starting our descent soon."

"That should give me time to read a few more pages before I have to put on my shoes and comb my hair," she said and turned back to the book on her lap, and his consequent impression that they were on somewhat different journeys persisted as they landed, deplaned, went through immigration, and reclaimed their baggage.

It might have been his distaste for sunburn that drew him to a customs line mostly of Mexicans, but whatever the reason, it hadn't been a shrewd choice. The returning gringos in the other lines moved along quickly, but the smaller duskier people ahead of him and Lucky were being quizzed and searched, and it looked as though they might be stalled indefinitely when a stack of meticulously ironed and folded shirts compressed into a small valise expanded uncontainably when the valise was opened. The owner of the shirts, a young man who said he was a student, was assisted by the man, woman, and child behind him in the line, and just in front of Ben and Lucky, in the slow furtive process of recompressing each shirt until the flimsy but inelastic valise could once more hold them. The helping family's containers then were both more extensive and more tentative. They had two vinyl cases, two shopping bags, and five cardboard cartons of different sizes tied with hairy brown cord each of which had to be opened with a lot of laborious untying of multiple knots. The cartons contained mostly kitchen equipment—round-bottomed aluminum pots, scorched earthenware, plastic dishes, wood and metal utensils. Nothing elicited any questions until the smallest box was opened and revealed four glass jars each in a vertical compartment. The inspector removed one jar and tilted it, and its tan contents moved in viscous slow motion behind the label that bore a picture of a goat's head with curled horns. "What's this stuff?" he asked with apparent revulsion.

"Is *cajeta*," the child said. She spoke toward her feet while her low-slung parents who had the hatchet features and pro-trusive bellies of the corn-eaters of the Yucatan and whose stiff, virulent green parkas showed vivid flashes of orange lin-ing, stood mute.

"What's that?" the inspector asked.

"*Cajeta*," she said again hopefully.

The inspector looked toward the rear of the hall for help, and as Ben followed his inquiring gaze he caught a glimpse of Sarah in the outer lobby, beyond a door that flapped open automatically when anyone approached it and shut again promptly when they'd passed through. She looked both be-mused and impatient, as though she was wondering how long it would take them to see her. Then, before he had time to share this discovery, Lucky's big leather shoulder bag jolted against his back. "It's really all right," she was saying with brisk reassurance as she worked her way around him. "The stuff's a kind of goat milk butterscotch. Kids spread it on bread, or even tortillas I suppose, like peanut butter. It may be murder on their teeth, but I'm sure it's otherwise harmless. If you get through all the fine print, I think you'll even discover that the milk it's made from has been pasteurized. I actually bought some once in the Haymarket, but I'm afraid I didn't like it."

The inspector brought the jar to his face with one hand and when he raised his glasses onto his forehead with the other to read the label, his eyes looked unexpectedly vulnerable, the soft skin around them dark and flaccid. "Right, *pasterizada*," he said after a moment of study, and let the glasses fall back into place.

"Finish?" the ancient child asked as the goat's head slid into its compartment once more.

She'd have looked even more homuncular if her parents had been somewhat taller, but her sturdy father wasn't more than five foot two or three, and the top of his wife's head came only to his nostrils as they stood pressed against each other waiting for the inspection to end. Then the three dun faces bent together to reassemble their goods, and wherever the light touched it strongly, their black hair showed identical rufous undertones, as though the hair contained blood. Their neat, firmly rounded bodies working efficiently and with little sound seemed designed on a more rational scale than the other, larger bodies crowding the room. "There is nothing else they have to do, is there?" Lucky asked, and when the inspector said there wasn't and she leaned forward to reassure the two adults and the child in the Spanish she'd studied in night school fifteen years back when she'd just begun to have Hispanic clients in the mental health clinic in which she worked, her purse struck Ben again, but in the ribs this time. Goaded by a sharp stab of pain, he was suddenly certain that the purse contained the ugly green squash she'd bought at the market in Oaxaca. She'd

said that she intended to take it home—to keep in the refrig-
erator for a while and then when the weather turned warm,
to see if she could get it to grow in a window box. After two
or three days of telling her that she wouldn't be allowed to
take it through customs and of being told that she'd manage
somehow, he'd stopped talking about it. But he hadn't stopped
thinking about it, and he'd have given odds now that this
unlikely vegetable that looked unfortunately like nothing so
much as a green scrotum was somewhere in the capacious
interior of that bag, cherished in one or more of the several
head scarves that were always in there. Cotton, but not in-
expensive and selected with decisive discrimination, these scarves
were one of several unexpected vanities Lucky harbored of
which only he knew the full obduracy. She was a lot less
consistent—and a lot more interesting consequently—than
anyone who didn't know her well could possibly have guessed.
But what was interesting about her could also be difficult, and
a surge of exasperation assailed him as he pictured this uncomfortably evocative object ensconced in that fair nest.

Now it was finally their turn to be checked out however,
and the customs inspector was asking how long they'd been
in Mexico, the purpose of their visit, whether they were bringing any agricultural products back with them, the total value
of the purchases they'd made. Asked perfunctorily, the questions were addressed to Ben only, and his suspicions were
exacerbated when he noticed that Lucky was content to let
him do all the answering. Ordinarily she'd have been sure to
complicate any such head-of-the-family routine, but now she'd
stepped behind him again with a deference that had to be false,
and was staring at the flapping door at the back of the room.
Every time the door opened, Sarah could be seen hanging back
a bit from the cluster of people just beyond the portals as she
followed their progress. Ben answered the succession of ques-

tions quickly and automatically, trying to slide over the moment when he might have been lying.

When they were passed along then without having to open any of their luggage, Lucky picked up her own bag, reasserting her competence, and hurried to the back of the room and out the automatic door. She dropped the bag to embrace Sarah, and Ben watched their obviously kindred bodies—Lucky's somewhat wider now at the hips than at the shoulders, and Sarah's already intimating that it would be in time—come together with an enviable absence of constraint. He wasn't of quite the same breed as these large-scale, handsome, uninhibited women. He'd put down his burdens too—the valise he held in his right hand and the briefcase he held in his left each weighted with books half of which as usual they'd never even opened while they were away—but even with his hands free he wouldn't when his turn came be able to throw his arms around Sarah the way Lucky had. His first impulse would be to get a full look at her, and when he did that some question was bound to occur to him and the moment for spontaneous greeting would be lost. And already, with her face still largely hidden from him, he was acutely aware of the familiarity of the way she was dressed. Lucky had worn sweaters and skirts like this when he'd first met her. She didn't any longer, hadn't for years, but Sarah had begun to wear them on Lucky's advice in her last year in law school, when she was interviewing for jobs.

Lucky released her, and when she turned toward him, he leaned forward and kissed her cheek. "Did you guys have a good time?" she asked, her voice registering both amusement and concern.

"I had a very good time," Lucky said. "By the second or third day I wasn't even worrying about Faith any more, because I knew you were here worrying about her for me, and

I'd entirely forgotten about all those other crucial matters that occupied me so frantically just before we left. Now I have to start trying to remember again what they were."

"That sounds pretty good," Sarah said. "How about you, Dad?"

"Since I didn't have as much to occupy me before we left, I had no opportunity to cleanse my mind as thoroughly as your mother did," Ben said. "But I enjoyed it anyway."

"Ah?" Sarah said. "You suffered no vacation from irony at any event."

"I'm not sure I was being ironic," Ben said. "But how were things here while we were gone?"

"Busy," Sarah said summarily and, he thought, evasively. "I'll bring your car around from the garage, and then on the way back I can catch you up a bit."

"We could walk to the garage," Lucky said. "We don't have all that much stuff to carry."

"Why should you?" Sarah said, and set out with a slight swagger, her left shoulder characteristically higher than the right.

"Do you think she really feels that chipper?" Lucky asked when she was out of earshot.

"I was wondering about that myself," Ben said, and then he said: "Tell me, did you have that damn vegetable in your purse the whole time?"

"I see no reason to tell you anything if you ask that way," Lucky said.

"I thought so," he said. "I kept picturing it swathed in soft cotton in there all the time I was lying to that guy."

"You only lied to him once," Lucky said, "and only one trivial lie. It would have been ridiculous not to have been allowed to bring it in. I can tell you for your ease of mind that I washed that damn vegetable as you call it in the hotel yesterday in some Clorox I got from the maid. Even if there were any live bugs on it before, they're dead bugs now. The maid of course thought I was crazy. I heard her giggling about it in the hall with a couple of the other maids. I endured ridicule from that nubile trio just to keep you more or less honest."

"Nonetheless," he said, "you might have let me know what you were up to."

"Up to?" she said. "Just the way you put it should tell you why I didn't. No crime has been committed. But if I had declared it, it would probably have been confiscated just because some designated dummy in the hall there was too ignorant to know it's perfectly harmless. Do you really want to discuss the matter any further?"

"I guess not," he said.

"We'd probably do well to get it settled before Sarah comes back. She wouldn't like hearing us go on about it, and I have the impression she has something on her mind she'd like to talk about if she judged the climate propitious."

"I got that idea too," he said, and under the kindlier influence of this common perception they settled to declare the matter resolved. This didn't mean however that there wasn't some festering potential still that might blow up later. Or that would, more likely, scar over. The age of their marriage could probably have been estimated by the number of such lesions, large and small, it had created. But they were both ready to pull together now in a common enterprise.

In the car though, Sarah showed no immediate inclination to say anything about herself. She ran down the family news, letting them know in more detail than there'd been in her first reassurance to Lucky that Faith had been reasonably well while they were away, and then that Mark had gotten the contract he'd been hoping for to remodel a row of tenements and that Phil's two kids had finally shucked off the flu bug they'd been passing back and forth between them since just after Christmas. All of this was reassuring, and though they'd known Sarah would keep track of Faith while they were away, they wouldn't necessarily have expected her to be in touch with both her brothers too in that relatively short time. Their three children had not seemed particularly closely allied to each other when they were young and living cheek by jowl, and it was pleasantly surprising to find that they were in more voluntary touch with each other now when they were scattered right across the country. Except that it also seemed another piece of evidence to Ben that he and Lucky had more limited function than they'd once had. That they were heading out to pasture.

Sarah's summary moved from her grandmother and her brothers to what was happening in her office to selected items of national and international news that she thought they'd want to know and might have missed. As she went on though, Ben was increasingly aware of some avoidance, something that she was moving around. For a while they even talked about the weather—how much less ice was on the river than had been there ten days before, but that winter was a residual leaden presence now instead of the series of brilliant phenomena it had been earlier. Then an ambulance was coming up the drive fast behind them, each oscillating blast of its siren closer than the last. Sarah eased the car right, and when Ben turned in the seat next to her to watch the blunt nose of the van with the reversed lettering under the windshield force a passage between the two lanes of traffic, he saw Lucky raise her eyebrows in what could have been recognition either of the insistent pressure of the ambulance or of the felt ellipsis in Sarah's narrative. Finally the ambulance passed them and Sarah picked up speed again, but they were crossing the bridge before she said, "The other thing you ought to know is that Carl's gone out of the country again for a while and we had such a fight about it this time that we may also have split. He's just about trashed the idea of getting that fellowship Dad put him onto, and he's on his way to Guatemala to do a stint in another one of those river blindness projects he's worked on before in various lousy parts of the world. This one's in some really godforsaken village that sounds like a perfect place to get killed. But I think I'm too pissed-off to say anything more about it."

They were almost home, and Sarah was slowing the car again. "You'll come up with us, won't you?" Lucky said.

"I don't think so," Sarah said, her voice as tight as it had been when she was a child and was too upset about something to risk crying by talking about it. "There's no place here to park, as usual, and anyway I still have some work to finish at the office. The best thing would be for me just to let you unload and then drop your car in the garage and get to the subway. I can phone you in the morning."

"I'll be back at work myself tomorrow," Lucky said.

"Okay, I can talk to Dad," Sarah said, sounding distinctly testy. But then she added, "Or of course I can call in the evening."

2

THIS WASN'T the first time Sarah and Carl had busted up or almost busted up, and it was hard to know therefore what weight to attach to her announcement. In the little more than three years they'd been living together, Carl's freelance work in public health had taken him out of the country frequently, mostly to northern Canada, but to Africa once also for six weeks, and to Central America more recently for almost a month. Each of these departures created a strain that had several times approached crisis proportions. And even when he wasn't away and was living with Sarah in her apartment in Somerville, there was something provisional about his presence there. He still hadn't given up his bachelor apartment in the South End. Because he'd had it for years, he said, it was dirt cheap, and it was useful to him as an office, convenient to the School of Public Health where most of his non-Canadian jobs originated and to the medical library. All of this was true, but it was easy to suppose that he was keeping the apartment as a fall-back position as well.

Their problem, Sarah said, wasn't so much that Carl couldn't find steady work somewhere in the United States where she could then find a job and follow him, as that he didn't really want to. That he liked being on the loose. She'd been surprised and pleased when he did decide to apply for one of the public health fellowships Ben had found out about from Charlie Coleman. If he was awarded one, that could almost certainly lead to the kind of a job that would make some reasonably ordinary version of marriage possible for them. And to a job that paid more probably than the jobs he was now getting came to cumulatively. But Sarah also suspected that deep down he really didn't wish his application to be successful, and she'd obviously now taken whatever it was exactly that had happened while Ben and Lucky were away as a demonstration that her suspicion was correct.

This difficulty of knowing just what had happened though had a somewhat different character for Lucky than it had for Ben. She'd been skeptical all along about Sarah and Carl's long-term prospects together. She didn't deny Carl's attractions. She claimed in fact to find him more attractive than Ben might necessarily wish to know and said she could certainly understand why Sarah was living with him. But she saw no future in it. Sarah wanted to be married, she said, and though Carl sometimes thought he did, other needs were always going to take precedence for him when the chips were down. "They really are just too different," she said again now when they were back in their apartment. "To put it crudely, he's not our kind. They're pulling in different directions too much of the time even when that isn't necessarily apparent. It's only because they're young that they even look probable together. I'm glad they haven't gotten married—and I can't tell you how many times I've thanked my stars that she hasn't gotten pregnant. I know how much she wants to have kids, but if they break up sooner rather than later, there'll be time still for her to fall for some nice guy instead of someone who's seductively impossible. Someone like her father for instance."

Ben looked uncomfortable, and she laughed and added, "Only a little tougher."

Laughter didn't do much though to mitigate the severity of that high-cheekboned, decisive face she'd inherited from her father, and that Sarah had then inherited from her with some mitigating roundness across the cheekbones that came from Faith. Lucky could be bruisingly clear-headed—maybe, Ben thought, because she really was tougher-minded than he was, readier to make hard choices. But given his feelings for and about Carl and about Sarah, it was impossible for him not to believe that together they'd constitute some kind of ultimate best combination—if, that is, they could make it together. However, before they'd gotten together, when each had been involved with a succession of other people, it would not have occurred to him to think of them together, and it gave him additional trouble when things weren't working out well between them to remember that it was he who'd first caused them to meet.

At exactly what historical moment had that meeting occurred? What glorious national episode, that is, did it accompany? There'd been so many of them in the past several decades—so many times when, pursuing his own life, he'd felt like a good German—that it was hard for him to be sure. Somewhere about the time of Cambodia though he thought. He remembered anyway that it had been in the fall, several years before they'd moved out of their old house into the apartment on the river. The immediate occasion had been the arrival in town of some high government official. He couldn't be certain any longer either just who it was, but thought probably Robert McNamara—now a latter day saint, but then a villain. Unaware of this inflammatory incursion, Lucky and he had planned to go to a concert that evening. Both boys were away by then—Phil was at Berkeley, and Mark had just gotten his first real construction job, also in California—and they were going to leave Sarah, who was then in high school, at home alone. But they never got to the concert, because right outside their door as they were leaving they found themselves between two opposing forces drawn up for battle. A squadron of cops in riot helmets with plastic visors were poised at the T where the street debouched onto Kirkland Street, and from the other end at Cambridge Street a clump of students in the padded parkas and navy pea jackets that were prescribed demonstration gear, some of them wearing football or motorcycle helmets too, were advancing provocatively. The police waited until they'd come a third or so of the way down the block, and then began to move too, but in formation, shoulder to shoulder. The students slowed, halted, threw a few rocks and bottles that clattered or shattered on the pavement. Then, when the police had continued to advance and were within thirty or forty feet of them, they broke, and retreated in notable disorder. The police then repaired to their previous position of readiness.

Ben and Lucky went back into the house and found Sarah already at the livingroom window to which she'd been drawn by the first burst of noise from the street. They joined her, to witness the same movements repeated a couple of times without significant variation. From the window however they could see only what happened at the climax, when the clash didn't take place and each side turned back, and frustrated by this limited view, Ben had soon gone out the side door and around the back of the house into the alley that led to the street. He'd promised Lucky and Sarah that he'd return soon to report whatever he saw or discovered, but he hadn't really gone out only to observe. He'd gone too because he thought the police were more likely to behave correctly if they were being watched by some older, interested non-combatants. Like a significant number of other citizens of his vintage in those years, he sometimes thought of himself as a guardian of a revolution he couldn't join.

The situation on the street when he got out there again was much what it had been when he'd been there before. The cops were once more at their corner, and though the number of students at the other corner might have increased somewhat, they were still only a raggle-taggle of skirmishers. By now though, the confrontation had been formalized, almost as though it were being staged. No cars were allowed into the narrow street, and both the students and the cops stayed on the macadam, leaving the brick sidewalks for the audience. And there was an audience, though it was very small. As Ben walked toward the students to get a closer look at them, he encountered several other observers one of whom told him that a coalition of student organizations had called for a picket line around a house just off the other side of Kirkland Street where a dinner was being given for the visiting dignitary, and that the police didn't intend to allow that. All the nearby side streets had been cordoned off, and there were cops out in force around the house as well to pick up anyone who managed to slip through the cordons.

When Ben got abreast of the students, a tall skinny boy carefully accoutred in a parka with a coyote collar and army surplus wool pants bloused into polished leather boots detached himself from the loosely constituted group and came to the curb. He affected a slouch and a slight drag of one foot, a veteran posture, but there was nothing affected about the unhealthy indoor pallor of his face. Despite the coolness of the evening too, moisture was visible on his temples and under his eyes where the wire frames of his glasses pressed against his skin. Supremely on edge, he'd begun to tell Ben even while he was still some distance from him what a dumb plan he and his fellow demonstrators had settled on. They should all have stuck together and marched straight up Kirkland Street from the Yard he said instead of breaking into small groups and trying to infiltrate by way of the side streets. On Kirkland

Street, even if the cops had prevented them from getting to the house that was their declared destination they'd have made some show. But fragmented as they were now, they were almost invisible, which made the whole enterprise both futile and dangerous. The cops, he said, were just going to play with them for a while, and then bust some heads.

He didn't look at Ben more than briefly as he talked to him. Most of the time his tensed eyes were directed toward the ground, and he was twirling a lock of light brown lank hair between a thumb and forefinger as he apparently pictured both the actual situation and its putative alternative. He was at once very nervous and very thoughtful, as though each state stimulated the other, and it might well have been this apparent wearing concurrence—the open way the boy let his feelings show and yet wasn't governed by them—that had captured Ben's attention in the first place, started that awareness of affinity and difference that was still both active and unsettled in his attitude toward Carl. Probably he hadn't at once made any conscious link to himself though, not certainly to his own time as a more conventional warrior when he'd more or less successfully though at great cost disguised even from himself just how nervous he was. Nervous? Too deeply fearful to admit even to himself how scared he was, and miserable. But this kid had been so openly as well as obviously nerved up that Ben found just watching him enervating. And suddenly he'd looked up and straight at Ben, his eyes squinting in what might have been pain, and asked him how he happened to be where he was.

Ben told him that he lived just down the street and that the commotion had brought him out. But then he added—idiotically he thought even as he did it—that he was also sympathetic to what the students were doing. The boy's eyes opened a bit further, but he didn't respond directly. Instead, he asked how long Ben thought it would be before the cops decided to bust some heads.

He panted slightly as he talked, and his attitude toward what might happen next reflected disgust as well as fear. They'd chosen a very bad spot on which to make a stand, he said. Another bunch of cops could easily move in behind them and cut off their retreat and they'd be trapped. What chance of success did Ben think they'd have though if they broke up and tried to get away through the back yards to either side of the street? Wouldn't it be hard for the cops to follow them there even if they wanted to, and wasn't it possible that some of them could slip off that way and get over to Kirkland Street where they ought to be?

Ben told him there were fences around most of the back yards, and moving through them with any speed therefore would be a difficult business at best. He didn't mention specifically that there was a six foot stockade fence around his own back yard and that at times he'd also wondered what he could do to it to make it cat proof. When the boy muttered something about bastions of privacy however, he did this as though quoting some well known judgment rather than expressing personal disapproval.

"Hey Carl," someone called then, and the boy excused himself and joined four or five other students, apparently the leadership group. They huddled together briefly in conference and then one of them announced to the group at large that they were once more going to try to break through the police formation. Carl hadn't been enthusiastic about that decision. Ben had heard him demurring, saying that it was silly to try something they'd gotten nowhere with several times already unless they thought they'd prove something by getting their heads broken. When he was overruled though, he gave tacit support to the recommendation and took a lead place in the advance.

This foray however was even more perfunctory than the previous ones had been. The students turned back before they'd gotten anywhere near the cops, and in the scramble, a girl tripped and fell and cut her wrist on a piece of broken bottle. Carl helped her tie a handkerchief around the cut, and then watched the dark stain that welled instantly through the white cloth with apparent fascination. "That looks real anyway, doesn't it?" he called over to Ben.

Shortly after this, Ben had gone back to the house as he'd promised he would to let Lucky and Sarah know what was happening, and as he got there he heard motorcycles moving down Kirkland Street winding their sirens. He figured that that must have been the guest of honor leaving the dinner, because suddenly the cops were no longer bent simply on containment. They advanced without waiting for provocation, brandishing their clubs with intent rather than as mere warning, and when the students turned this time they continued to pursue them. They ran like men who didn't like to run, a heavy reluctant motion that had to generate anger, and the thud of their boots against the street made the house tremble.

This time too they didn't return. A couple of squad cars moved across the end of the street instead to hold the position for a while, and the rattle of their radios was audible in the house. Ben went out the side door again to see what had happened, and found Carl sitting on the steps with his head in his hands. The police had clubbed him down, he said, but left him where he fell, and when he picked himself up and saw the squad cars move in ahead of him, cutting off escape in that direction, he ran into the alley he'd seen Ben turn into a few minutes before and found his way from there into the yard.

At first he'd refused Ben's invitation to come inside. He said he only wanted to take a short rest, and then see if he couldn't get to the house where the dinner party was going on by way of the back streets after all. He wouldn't mind being arrested once he got there. That would be visible and might even get into the papers. It only bugged him he said to let the cops club him in private on a side street.

He didn't look capable of walking another hundred feet even if there were no fences to scale along the way. But he was determined to try, and not ready to give up at first even after Ben had told him he thought the party was probably over, that when the police had rushed the demonstrators just now, that had been their way to call it a night. The logic of this got to him only slowly, almost certainly because he had another scenario vividly fixed in his mind. But the strength of his resistance to the idea of taking shelter in the house must also have been a measure of how much that was what he wanted to do. It was bull-headed resistance to inclination. And when he did come into the kitchen finally—though he was scared, exhausted, and in some pain—he talked a brilliant mixture of bravado and skepticism almost non-stop for the best part of the next couple of hours. Sarah, who was then seventeen, sat opposite him at the kitchen table the whole time, silent and rapt as Desdemona listening to a pale Othello, Ben had thought, though he knew also that both sides of this analogy were way off, and that he was certainly no Brabantio. It hadn't even seemed funny to Sarah as it had to him and Lucky that Carl had refused either coffee or whiskey, but drank milk and munched Oreo cookies instead as he talked. Nor that he was wound up so tight he had a nose bleed. He continued to talk though even with his head over the back of the chair while Lucky held a towel full of ice cubes pressed against his nostrils.

3

"SARAH DIDN'T say anything to you did she about someone you apparently knew once named I think Marvin Traglich? Is that right? Originally Traeglich, I suppose. He seems to have touched off this disturbance."

The way Faith offered this, at once tentative and precise, might have sounded disingenuous if Ben hadn't known how convinced she was that she was losing her memory. He didn't think she was, but she was slipping too much in other ways for him to be able to dismiss that conviction as fantasy. There'd been some further attenuation, some increased ghostliness, in just the short time he'd been away. And yet she had stored away and then produced Marvin Traglich's name, and he was entirely disposed to credit her belief that it was important. Just hearing Marvin mentioned again had sent a shot of ice water into his vascular system.

Faith's instincts had always been dependable, which was one more reason why knowing she wouldn't be with them much longer unsettled him too and not just Lucky. She wasn't his mother, and he'd reached an age himself by which, if they get there, most men have either learned how to proceed on their own or discovered anyway that they must. But his case was special. He traced everything that was distinctive about his life to Faith. All the ways he, Lucky, and their children dealt with each other were shaped by emulation. What they'd learned from Faith though, she'd mostly discovered for herself. And it was because of this, because they weren't genetic possessions but were perpetuated instead by emulation, that he too and not just Lucky or Phil or Mark or Sarah could derive from Faith. He wasn't reborn exactly when he and Lucky were married, but he was reconceived. There were also limits of course to the power of emulation, but it was only after he'd known Lucky for a while that he'd been able even to imagine a life significantly influenced by choice. The world he was born to had been governed by prescription. Notions of the desirable were monolithic, and the question wasn't what you were to do, but only whether you could do it.

Even Lucky's derivation from her mother though was both by emulation and by reaction which was the flip side of emulation. To Faith's eyes, the life she, and he then with her, had elected looked rather constrained, as she felt free to let them know from time to time. Sarah though was something of a reversion. She had more again of Faith's expansive sense of possibility. More too than either of her brothers had. This double possibility, of emulation and reaction, had made their three children a remarkably diverse lot. His mother-in-law had lived a far chancier life than Lucky or he had wanted or attempted, and Sarah had a taste for her boldness. Whether she also had the constitution for it though was not yet clear.

Perhaps because of this affinity, Sarah sometimes confided in Faith when she was being reserved still with him and Lucky, and since she'd been living in their apartment with Faith for the past ten days, there'd been more opportunity than usual for this kind of confidence. It wasn't only because Faith might have some light to shed on what had been going on between Sarah and Carl however that Ben had come in to see her this afternoon. He'd have felt deprived if the day had gone by and he hadn't spent some time with her. He and Lucky had looked in on her briefly when they got back the previous afternoon, and then Lucky had had a somewhat longer visit with her before going to work this morning. But he knew she'd prefer a visit from him after Annie Ryerson had been in to help her bathe and dress, and he'd arranged his day accordingly.

He'd arrived at the library promptly at nine, impatient to feel purposeful again after ten days of leisure which had begun to feel enforced before it was concluded. Until they'd gone to Mexico, ever since late November, he'd been spending a couple of days each week reading at the Public Library. He'd chosen to read there rather than at the Athenaeum where a friend had offered to put him up for membership. He'd always admired the handsome building on Copley Square with its long, low, confident neo-classic facade, and though the massive new addition didn't achieve comparable dignity, he very much liked the way it was being used. The friend who'd suggested the Athenaeum had warned him that though the Public Library was indeed full of books, the books he'd want or need on any given day were very likely not to be available. This wouldn't be true, he'd said, at the Athenaeum, and for anyone doing research therefore who didn't have access to Widener, or didn't like sitting in a reading room full of kids, it was more than worth what it cost to join.

It wasn't the cost however that had kept Ben from embracing this opportunity. It was his uncertainty about just what it was he was going to be doing, and his certainty that whatever it was wouldn't merit being called research. After more than thirty years of dealing with books relatively few of which he found time to read, for some months now he was going to spend a large part of each day reading. Or was going to do this if he could. Habituated to a more active life, he wasn't sure his flesh or his spirit could accommodate to sitting in one place for very long, and when he wasn't testing this at home, when he needed some change of scene or some book he didn't own, the Public Library seemed the right resource. He'd feel more nearly comfortable there, under less pressure anyway to fly false colors. And despite his friend's warning, maybe because his interests weren't very recondite, most of the books he wanted turned out to be available when he wanted them. That morning he'd requested two books and gotten both, and he'd read for about as long as he could anyway without interruption when it was time to quit and go home to see Faith.

One of the chief attractions of the apartment he and Lucky had bought when they sold their house was that part of it could be divided off to make a small independent apartment for Faith. Independent but accessible. It had its own separate entrance, but there was also a communicating door between the two apartments for emergencies. Faith could no longer live safely or easily by herself, but she couldn't relinquish independence easily either, and this was therefore an ideal arrangement. And that the house despite its size hadn't lent itself to anything comparable made the move a positive step as well as a retreat.

He got back to the apartment a little before two after stopping on the way for a sandwich and a cup of coffee. By two he figured, Faith would have read the newspaper and her mail, written some letters, bathed and dressed and had lunch with Annie's help. She'd be ready therefore for some sociability. Only Manfred Fox must have been familiar with this timetable too, for he was already with her when Ben arrived.

Manfred was an English Jew from Nottingham who'd come to the States for a visit when he was quite young and managed never really to leave again. He had family money, and though he'd worked from time to time over the years, he'd always been first and foremost a man of cultivation. This evidenced itself in matters of food, drink, dress, and the arts, about the current state of which he was always knowledgeable. When he had worked, the work had always had something to do with music. But Manfred was also a living demonstration of the disposition of money to go to money. In the late 50's, he'd started a small company to record baroque music performed on baroque instruments, and it was soon successful enough to be bought out handsomely by a major European recording company.

Sometime after Lucky's father died, Manfred had courted Faith for a while. Lucky remembered him then as something of a dandy. Probably, she thought, he'd wanted Faith to marry him, and probably she'd turned him down, but Lucky and her sister both assumed that they'd been lovers. Lucky was ten when her father died and her sister was twelve, and in the next decade or so her mother—who'd been the principal of a small private girls' school—had had several lovers she thought, and probably more than one chance to remarry. She'd apparently had no interest in marrying again however, though she was interested in men. Eventually Manfred had married someone else and dropped out of sight, but when his wife died many years later he'd reappeared as a rather spent version of the dandy he'd once been. Faith had retired by that time, and once a week or so, until she'd had the fall that crippled her, he'd take her to a show or concert if there was something in town that met his standards, or else to some good restaurant for lunch or dinner. Since her fall though, Faith had declined to go out at all, except to Friends meetings on those Sundays when Lucky could go with her. She didn't choose to be seen walking down one of the long aisles at Symphony Hall or at the Colonial or the Shubert with a four-clawed metal cane, and it made no encouraging difference to her to know that there were always women and men her age or younger frequenting the concert halls and theatres with canes and even in wheelchairs. She remembered only as cautionary the dowager whose chauffeur had for years wheeled her into Symphony every Friday afternoon and then unrolled a wire with a microphone at the end of it from the hearing aid built into her chair down an aisle almost to the stage.

Having always been gregarious though, she craved visitors now, and she was audibly delighted when Ben phoned to ask if he could come across to see her. She didn't mention however, presumably not to discourage him, that Manfred was with her already, and his distinctive face registered his disappointment when Ben appeared. Manfred had sanguine, almost purple, corrugated skin, and its darkness was intensified by a carefully trimmed beard that was still inky black though the residual fringe of hair around his bald head was grizzled. Tufts of equally black hair also projected over his eyes and thronged his nostrils. He was a kindly and attentive man, but he was also a heavy, and Faith seemed to enjoy the idea of his visits more than she did the visits themselves. She was probably counting on Ben's arrival to encourage Manfred not to stay too much longer, but he tried before he left to persuade her to make an exception to her general practice and go with him the following week to an exhibition of Chinese bronzes at the Museum of Fine Arts that he referred to as "an event of the greatest cultural importance."

Since he'd had Parkinson's, his always measured speech had become even more pronouncedly measured, presumably to minimize the disposition of his voice to tremble, and he camouflaged other symptoms in studied fashion too. Whenever possible, he kept his hands locked one to the other or in his pockets, and he affected an ascot to cover a pulse in the hollow of his throat. Today the ascot was paisley, which went well with his herringbone jacket, gray flannels, and black loafers.

Faith though was wearing a house dress, opaque stockings, and tennis sneakers, and was three-quarters enclosed anyway by the narrow, high-backed wing chair in which she now spent most of the day and, when she was in too much pain to sleep, a considerable part of the night too. Her four-clawed cane stood by her, next to the chair.

Ben had seen her ensconced this way so frequently lately, that it no longer made her look obviously invalided. The chair had become her ambience. And though she'd wasted away dramatically—in part it seemed by plan since she ate very little—she was still wonderfully attractive. Her skin was a mere translucence however over the rounded bones of her face, and he had to remind himself that she'd once had the kind of firm rosy flesh that stimulates appetite. Her face had lengthened too as it thinned, and this was accentuated when she sacrificed the braids that had met before in a coronet across the top of her head. When she fell, she'd cracked a couple of vertebrae and her right hip, and Lucky and Ben found her at four o'clock in the morning, after she'd telephoned for help, sitting on the floor with her back propped against the telephone table, in pain but also vividly angry. She'd been stupid she said, holding herself to account, and when she decided while she was convalescing after the hip had been pinned that she was never again going to be able to hold her arms above her head long enough to braid her hair, she declared that the braids had to go. Whatever there was to say for this decision practically, it smacked too of self-punishment, but after trying unsuccessfully to dissuade her from it, Lucky had agreed to do what she wished. Not only were the braids to come off it developed, but her hair was to be cropped short all over. She wanted a crew cut, she said, because that would require minimum care. She'd had something very particular in mind, and Lucky had worked slowly under her instruction, taking off no more hair at any one cut or in any one place than she was certain she'd been told to take. After every few cuts too she'd put down the comb and scissors and hold up a couple of facing mirrors so that Faith could see what had been done and say what she wanted done next. It was a painstaking process, but since it had been done Faith had expressed no regrets unless her periodic assertions of how much easier it was to have her hair short could be construed as indirect statements of regret. To Ben however she still looked shockingly shorn at times, like an elderly Joan of Arc.

An imperious one though too. When she saw that Manfred felt unwanted and was preparing to leave, she pressed him to stay for a cup of tea and pressed Ben into service to make it. Each did what was asked of him too without demur, but this didn't take very long, and within half an hour Manfred had shuffled off anyway, a lot less imposing on his feet than when he was seated.

Having disposed of him with some amenity, Faith settled herself to talk. "You enjoyed yourselves down there I gather," she said, so unemphatically that it could have been either a statement or a question.

"Sure," Ben said, "though as usual I sometimes found having to have a good time a burdensome assignment. Lucky's always better at that."

"I was never much of a one for vacations myself," Faith said. "Except when Margaret and Lucky were young, when I'd just be doing what I did at other times anyway in less convenient circumstances. Lucky takes after her father in that regard. He had a talent for letting go whenever he had the chance."

Recently, when she recalled her husband who had been dead for going on half a century, she'd talked about him with a kind of detachment that gave Ben a somewhat fuller picture of the successful but ill-fated physician who'd been Lucky's father than he'd ever had before. But she'd also been mentioning him more frequently recently, as though without much room to think her way forward, she was doing a lot of going back instead. "It's an enviable talent," Ben said. "It doesn't even, as I once liked to think, require stupidity."

"But it can sometimes be hard to watch in action anyway," she said, "if you have less of that talent yourself."

"Exactly," he said. "And while we were gone I also rather lost track of what was going on around here."

Doubt clouded Faith's face now, which he took to mean that she knew he was referring to something specific but wasn't sure what it was. "You mean with the kids?"

"Yeah."

"I'm not entirely clear about that either."

"You know Carl has apparently left town suddenly. For Guatemala."

"I do know that," she said.

"Sarah was pretty upset when she talked about it, driving us home from the airport yesterday. Not that she talked about it very much."

"I'm sure she is upset," Faith said, "only I don't believe she's simply desolate. I'm not sure you and Lucky realize what special creatures you are. Having been happily monogamous all your lives gives you a somewhat skewed view of average human possibility. And of what Sarah may be feeling right now. After all, if something really has occurred, it hasn't just happened to her. She was the one who insisted on putting the big meaning on whether Carl did or didn't take this job, on making it a decisive act. He thought he was only doing what he'd done some number of times before, and doing it this time to keep his alternatives open if the fellowship didn't come through. Sarah's a tough person, and no matter how bad she feels right now, she'll be all right again after a while however they do or don't work it out."

Faith's opinion didn't surprise Ben, but it isolated him. Though arrived at on a very different basis, effectively it had a lot in common with Lucky's. She too was ready to look on Carl as a passing figure in Sarah's life. "You may be right," he said, "but she certainly didn't sound too great yesterday."

"What exactly did she say?"

"Not much, beyond saying what had happened and that she wasn't up to talking about it. That's what troubled me."

"She's probably still too angry to talk about it."

"I guess that's what she did say."

"Of course," Faith said.

As her face thinned, the skin had paled and contracted until it looked like fine-lined parchment except over her cheekbones where an opaque, somewhat fleshier patch brightened when she was excited or amused. These two patches had begun to glow now, and Ben could also hear her amusement when she said, "Are you brooding about something? Some possibility? What is it? Helping them?"

The succession of questions was at least mildly derisive, and Ben said cautiously, "I'm not sure. Maybe. I'd have to find out more about what's happened first and I thought you might know."

"Remember that Carl's probably the one you'd have to help," she said, "and that would be tricky. He has, as you know better than I, a mixed history that can't be ascribed only to accident, and he also doesn't wear his talents inconspicuously or suffer fools kindly. All of which he understands but doesn't necessarily wish to change. He apparently believes there's some vendetta in progress against him that's just about certain to cost him that fellowship, which he applied for mostly I'd guess at Sarah's urging and on which their chief chance for a changed life seems to depend. Sarah though suspects that he has a deep wish to believe in this vendetta, and that the wish outweighs the evidence. Or even that the wish has caused something to happen that needn't otherwise have happened. She's not entirely consistent about what she thinks, probably again because she's so angry. But she's sure anyway that saying he won't get the fellowship and that he should have known better than to apply for it in the first place is Carl's way of telling her to stop trying to arrange his life for him the way she'd like it to be."

"Has Carl talked to you about it?" Ben asked.

"No, he hasn't, but there hasn't been much chance for him to either. I didn't see him very often while they were living here. The very good care Sarah was taking of me was largely without his assistance."

Faith offered this information too with a certain amount of throwaway amusement, as though it shouldn't be a surprise. When Ben asked her if she knew exactly what had caused Carl to decide that something fishy was going on however, her amusement disappeared and she turned palpably anxious. She thought she should know, she said. Very possibly she had known once and had forgotten. She could forget almost anything these days. But then almost without pause she told him about Marvin Traglich and Ben assured her that Traglich might very well have been the cause. That that sounded only too probable.

4

BEN REALLY needed to act or do, and found it hard sometimes to curb this need long enough to let thought have its say. When Faith told him she believed Marvin Traglich was the instigator of the trouble between Carl and Sarah, he was ready to get in touch with Marvin at once to find out what was going on, and recognized then only reluctantly that it would be a mistake to do this without speaking to Carl or Sarah first.

He had neither the disposition nor the habits of a thinker, and the contemplative life he was now leading could make him very uneasy. It was only four months since he'd ceased to be the owner of a bookstore in Cambridge and the three branch stores in Brookline, Newton, and Wellesley that it had spawned. He'd sold them to a large chain that had been trying to buy him out for some time, and the sale had taken place almost exactly thirty-five years after he'd taken his first bookstore job, in Boston, just after the war.

That had been a decisive move too. Not only was Boston Lucky's city—he'd grown up in and around New York—but if he hadn't gotten married during the war, his life would almost certainly have been very different. He would probably have gone on to graduate school on the G.I. Bill when he got out of the army and ended up a professor of English or history. In 1946 though, when he and Lucky had been married for three years of which they'd spent less than six months together, graduate school seemed a possibility he'd overrun even though that was where most of his friends, some of them also married, headed when they got out of the service. He'd decided without much agonizing to get a job instead, so that he and Lucky could start having a family. To do this, and to do it in Boston rather than New York, was to acknowledge what he thought he was doing anyway when he married Lucky. He was placing their life together under her auspices.

He'd begun clerking at the bookstore in the financial district in early 1946, and by the summer of 1947 he'd become assistant manager of the store and figured he'd learned enough about the book business to justify borrowing money from his father to buy the Phoenix, a bookstore near Harvard Square that was of no particular distinction except that it was small and in a good location and was one of the few bookstores in the Boston area that stocked remainders. The store had never shown much profit, and though he continued to stock remainders, he also began to carry quality paperbacks just as the quality paperback business began to expand rapidly. That had been either beginner's luck or obvious logic, but it had at any event rapidly increased his volume of business, and he did well then also with magazines, quality greeting cards, and calendars. He'd opened his first branch store, in Belmont, in 1955, and in 1957, by which time he and Lucky had three children, he was able to buy a house in Cambridge just before the prices of houses began to skyrocket. He was no tycoon, but he'd made a modest success in a necessarily modest business at a time when there was a lot of money around, and by the time there was less and starting out would have been a lot tougher, he was established. Only eventually, as the business grew larger and more successful, he was no longer enjoying it very much.

In the last couple of years, he'd wondered at times whether

there really wasn't something else he could do. He didn't think he'd made a mistake by doing what he'd done when he did it. By and large he believed he'd always chosen pretty well among his options, and that to second guess them now in retrospect would be an exercise in forgetfulness and futility. It had taken him a while though to discover that he had all the basic attributes for business except the right libido. Success never pleased him very much except when it translated into immediate, concrete advantage. He'd enjoyed having a business that prospered and had few problems, so that he could leave it at the end of the day and return to the comfortable, busy, and interesting household that it made possible. But as his children started to leave home—and even more markedly when they left school and became self-sufficient—that translation became harder and harder to effect. He was making more money than he needed, and the discrepancy would have been even more apparent if, almost as though to hide this, he wasn't also spending his money in ways that meant little to him, like buying a Volvo when the Plymouth station wagon he'd had for ten years died, or upgrading the kinds of hotels Lucky and he stayed in when they took vacations he didn't necessarily enjoy much anyway.

Lucky had been working for some years now too, and her salary, though not large, increased their affluence. But he knew that she'd have gone on doing just what she was doing even if she'd been paid less. Day after day she was dealing with people who were in trouble, and at least some part of the time she thought there was something to be done for them and that she did it better than it would have been done by someone else. She would even say just that. And also that it was a way to pay for her own good fortune. The attention she gave to her work sometimes seemed excessive to him and even self-deluding, and he saw too that it consumed a lot of the finite energy and attention of which he might otherwise have had larger benefit. But her example had had more influence than he'd have wanted her to know on his decision to sell his business. The opportunity to sell on terms somewhat more favorable than a previous bid he'd turned down not too long before coincided this time with a surprise offer of a job at Huntington Community College. A relatively new school, right in downtown Boston, Huntington served a constituency very similar to the one from which Lucky's clients were drawn.

He was going to Huntington as an administrator, but Charlie Coleman had told him that he could do some teaching too after a while if he wished. Charlie, who was the president of Huntington, had been a regular customer at the Phoenix for most of the time Ben owned it, and over the years the two of them had become friends. When Charlie came into the store to buy a book, he'd generally go back to Ben's office to chat for a while too. They might talk about almost anything, but since Charlie's curiosity about how things worked was always active, he'd frequently ask questions about the store which Ben was glad to answer or consider, knowing that Charlie was then likely to come up with some useful observation or suggestion.

Charlie's intelligence was wonderfully uninhibited. He could apply himself to almost anything. He'd worked for the Commonwealth in several different capacities and he'd been a shrewd choice to get Huntington started when education in the inner city became a hot issue. After five years, the school had grown so much that he needed someone he could trust and get along with to help him run the place, and he'd just gotten the okay to hire an administrative vice president when he came into the Phoenix one late afternoon the previous September and Ben told him about the new offer he'd just had from Brandt Corporation. Charlie listened attentively, but surprised Ben by expressing no opinion as to whether or under what circumstances the Brandt offer ought to be considered seriously. Two days later however he told Ben he'd have a job for him at Huntington if he did decide to sell.

The timing was perfect. The Brandt offer would have been too good to disregard anyway if Ben hadn't been so sure that retirement wouldn't suit him. He was neither a natural contemplative nor a happy idler. Whatever he might have become once, what he was now had been shaped by the life he'd led. His developed capacities were all for doing, and the idea of doing something he hadn't done before was very attractive. A new job would have its hazards too of course. He couldn't know how adaptable he was any longer. He'd been doing the same thing for a long time and also running his own show. But if the job at Huntington didn't work out, he could at any event quit it without much financial risk. The terms of the Brandt sale were good enough, he figured, to take care of him and Lucky for the rest of their lives, which was an enviable but also a somewhat daunting prospect.

It had taken less than two weeks to conclude the agreement with the Brandt people, and things progressed so quickly thereafter that by the middle of November the business was out of his hands. His job at Huntington wouldn't come into existence until July however, which meant that he had half a year to spend as he wished. Or could. He'd had very few plans. He was going to begin to read for and think about a couple of courses he might teach, and in June he was signed up to take a one-month cram course for new college administrators at the Harvard Business School. But this didn't add up to a schedule, and he'd be discovering therefore what it was like to wake up in the morning with little or nothing to do unless he could think of something he chose to do.

Not since his college vacations had he had to decide how he was going to spend each day without the constraints and guidance of large obvious tasks that demanded doing, and then judge too at the end of the day whether he had in fact done anything. The requirement of justification was as imperious now as it had been then, but the criteria were even less defined and, for that reason, less susceptible to realization. He'd had plenty of time in the past several months to become familiar with the dissatisfactions that can accrue to a fortunate life. Or, more particularly, the dissatisfactions that his fortunate life had been storing up for him. But his life hadn't simply been fortunate. He felt frequently that it hadn't quite been earned, that he'd scarcely had to fight for it, that it had more or less fallen to him. For years he'd been troubled recurrently by this suspicion of not quite having won what he had, which must have had something to do with why he was so vulnerable to fears of catastrophic loss. That something might happen to Lucky or to one of their children. Or to his business, though this had been a lesser worry. What he hadn't thought much about however was the natural attrition to which his fortunate life was inevitably subject. He'd constructed no buffers to non-essentiality, to becoming an observer rather than a participant, to the varying aspects of common sadness. He hated common sadness. Anticipatable, it should also he thought have been endurable if he hadn't been too stupid to anticipate it. If he hadn't had his mind on the wrong hazards. And even if he hadn't had to fight for his fortunate life, there had to be some way to fight now not to feel that he'd lost it, that there was nothing more for him to do or want. Only the fight metaphor still didn't seem quite cogent to him, mostly because he couldn't even now define an opponent, identify an enemy.

Even the avowed and relatively definable part of what he'd been doing recently, the reading for the two courses one on voyage literature and one on autobiography that he thought he'd like to teach at Huntington, could sometimes lend unmeetable urgency to this question. Just before he'd gone to Mexico, he'd been reading Chekhov's *Journey to Sakhalin* on the assumption that it would probably be suitable for one or the other of his projected courses, and it had been reassuring to have that assumption turn out to be correct. The book however was unsettling. "Please don't place great literary hopes on my Sakhalin trip," Chekhov writes to his friend Ivan Scheglov before departing. "I'm not going for observations or impressions; all I want to do is live six months differently from the way I've lived before." A little earlier he'd written even more modestly: "Granted I may get nothing out of it, but there are sure to be two or three days out of the whole trip that I'll remember all my life with rapture or bitterness." And only two months later, after a week spent on a boat on the Omur River, he can already "truly state that after seeing such riches and experiencing so many delights I am now not afraid of dying." Twice the age Chekhov had been when he wrote this, Ben, reading it, was about to go briefly to a luxury hotel in a provincial city in Mexico overrun by pleasure seekers where he certainly wouldn't, for example, make vigorous outdoor love to half-savage women as Chekhov had done in the course of his hazardous and uncomfortable journey. Any adventures he had were going to be pretty interior, and it was hard to see how they could answer to any of the needs to which his free time was giving remarkable exigence.

The trip to Mexico had in fact been little but an interruption, and now that he was home again he intended to spend as much of every day as he could, reading to save his life. That could frequently feel promising, but the promises couldn't be fulfilled on the printed page alone, and he anticipated a lot of cycling between hope and the familiar common sadness he detested.

For the first few days after his return, he found himself

reading with exhilaration a large proportion of the time. On Sunday morning however when he didn't settle down to read, that exhilaration suddenly had no carry-over. He couldn't retain the affect of his reading the past few days, and he felt not just unemployed, but unemployed in a way that risked consequences. As though he wasn't just doing nothing that mattered, but also neglecting some unknown but assigned task. It didn't help at all to know that this had to be a notion without foundation, and when Faith and Lucky departed for the Friends meeting, he was awash in bleakness that seemed to emanate from the residual impression in his hands and arms of Faith's material absence. He'd helped her down in the elevator, and then through the long corridor in the cellar and up a short flight of stairs to the back street behind the apartment house, and when he'd closed his hand around her wrist to hold her, for an instant that had seemed much longer he thought it might continue to close until there was nothing between the middle finger and its opposing thumb but the stuff of her coat. In the three weeks since he'd last helped her this way, while he was doing nothing, she'd diminished appreciably. He finally found the thin spindle of her wrist, but her weight on his supporting arm was trivial. They'd had to do this passage too in stages, stopping frequently to rest, the last time on the sidewalk only a few feet from where Lucky was parked waiting for them. Fortunately at the other end of the short trip, in the park that had once been Henry Wadsworth Longfellow's front lawn, there'd be a lot less distance to negotiate.

Faith didn't go to meeting every Sunday, but she counted on being able to go occasionally and Lucky counted on going with her. As they departed this morning though, Ben wondered why he hadn't joined them. He'd do nothing after all while they were gone but wait to be downstairs again when they returned so he could help Faith out of the car and up to her apartment once more. Watching them recede into the distance—the backs of their heads in similar knitted hats, one gray and the other black, visible through the rear window of the car—he was startled by how wan he felt. They were going to be back after all in less than two hours. And it was because he'd so rarely chosen to join them in the past that they no longer asked him if he wished to. Only it seemed odd to him now that he didn't. He wasn't after all a practicing Jew. But he was apparently committed to being a non-practicing Jew and nothing else. He'd given up active adherence to the faith to which he was born, but he wasn't going to take on even minimal adherence to any substitute faith either. Why should he be so absolute about that though? He had no negative convictions about Lucky's inobtrusive but persistent Quakerism. Nor about Faith's, which was more conspicuous. He even connected a simplicity they could both manage in recognizably similar fashion, and that he rarely attained himself but wished he could more often, with Quakerliness. Part of what Lucky had learned from Faith and not reacted against had to be related to the route her mother had followed first to the Ethical Culture Society when she was a child in New York, and then, in her late teens when she'd come to Boston to go to college, to the Society of Friends. She'd no longer found any sufficiency in that earlier choice made for her by her parents in the course of what she called their move from Judaism to gentility. She made similar remarks of course about the Quakers. Some of her best Friends were Jews. Probably only Quakers trembled before no one. Only within the Society could you partake of so much moral prosperity. But what was different was that these quips of varying age and originality were never dismissive.

Ben had on occasion gone to a Friends meeting, and he'd found each occasion congenial. There'd been moments when he'd been positively happy to be where he was, and that hadn't been the case at all with any of the return visits to synagogues he'd made under some special compulsion after his departure at the same uncompromising age at which Faith had decamped from the Ethical Culture Society. His difficulties on each of these returns had been immediate, physical, animal. He'd found himself gasping for air. But he was also pretty sure that his moments of contentment sitting on a hard bench in a bright wintry meeting room warmed by a log fire didn't add up to anything he could sustain. In any retrospect, he found the Friends, however admirable, significantly funnier than Faith found them.

On this particular Sunday morning though, he might have done well to go again nonetheless. It wouldn't really have been a new testing of the waters, but it could have been an agreeable way not to be at bleak loose ends for the next couple of hours. Incomparably better, he thought, to be sitting between Faith and Lucky in the populated quiet of a bright bare room, with the quiet broken from time to time by speech, by the rustle of clothing, by the occasional crackling of a large log burning in the fireplace. The warmth and the small social sounds would have been at a good remove from that arctic region of the mind into which he'd suddenly and unexpectedly descended. He could think of no way to make an opportunity of the next couple of hours, and the Sunday papers lying in a thick wad in the livingroom when he went back upstairs seemed exactly what he didn't need.

It felt like rescue therefore when he heard the door to the apartment open and was pretty sure it was Sarah who'd opened it even before she called "Hello." Then when he called back that he was in the livingroom, she said, "I thought I'd probably find you here."

His mood must have been audible, for the trace of a smile

on her face when she came into the room was at once inquiring and mildly teasing. "I suppose Mom took Faith to meeting and left you here alone," she said.

"That's right," he said, "and you see me not making much of my solitude."

"Well, I'll join you in a minute," she said, "and you'll no longer be in solitude."

This was the first time he'd seen Sarah since she'd picked them up at the airport. Lucky had talked to her a couple of times on the telephone, but said she couldn't tell much from that. The way she looked and sounded now however seemed, whatever else, to justify Faith's confidence in her resilience. He heard her walk into the kitchen, and when she returned she was carrying a cup of coffee and had shed her coat. She was dressed for Sunday in patched jeans, a maroon velour jersey that had lost its nap in several places, and blue sneakers with holes through which the darker blue of her tights was visible. "Coffee's just what I needed," she said. "It's pretty raw out there today."

"And you're all but barefoot," he said. "No one would know you were a big shot lawyer making a big salary."

"Come on, Dad," she said. "Maybe that's just what I don't want them to know. And anyway, I manage to dress myself every day without help."

"I'm sure," he said.

She slumped onto a chair opposite him, and stretched out her legs so that they spanned most of the space between them. More a posture of relaxation than the real thing though, he thought, given the way she was scrutinizing him across the rim of the cup cradled between her palms. Sometimes his daughter's boldness could seem ruthless to him—which he knew by now was likely to mean that she was pushing the limits of her capacity for boldness in principle. "You're holding out on me," she said, and stretched one leg further to tap her foot against his ankle.

"Am I?" he said. "About what?"

"Faith tells me she introduced Marvin Traglich's name into a conversation the two of you had about me and Carl, and that you seemed to attribute unhappy importance to it. Why haven't I heard about that from you?"

"We haven't talked since I talked to Faith," he said, "and also I thought I should wait for you to introduce the subject. But Faith's right. Though I hate to rock your boat any more than it's rocking already, I have to say that I consider Marvin an uncertain element."

"It doesn't seem to be a very stable boat, does it?" she said.

He said he was sorry, which brought conversation to a more abrupt conclusion than either of them desired. He hadn't meant to sound perfunctory, and he didn't believe she'd introduced the matter only for the satisfaction of having him admit that he and Faith had indeed had some exchange about it. But for the moment, though they continued to watch each other eloquently, this was where they were. Then Sarah began again with a question. "What did Faith actually say to you about Marvelous Marvin?"

"That he probably set off the trouble between you and Carl."

"That's true as far as it goes," she said, "but I'd distribute the blame a bit. I've been pushing my luck with Carl. In various ways. A relatively minor instance is that we only ran into Marvin because I dragged him to a party he'd been smart enough not to want to go to. One of the lawyers in the office gave it, to celebrate becoming a partner. The place was lousy with big shots and would-be big shots among whom Marvin, whom neither Carl nor I had seen for years, was of course right at home."

"And it was there that he told you that Carl was the object of some kind of investigation?"

"He told me nothing," Sarah said. "I never really talked to him. But he was the only other person at the party Carl knew, and so Carl did talk to him. Talked to him a lot to my astonishment, until the conversation broke off abruptly. I was watching when that happened, and I thought from the way Carl turned away and walked into another room, that something uncongenial had occurred. Were they good friends when they knew each other back in college?"

"I doubt it," Ben said. "They saw something of each other certainly, but I can't imagine that they were ever very congenial."

"That would be my hunch too," Sarah said. "I gathered from what Carl told me when we got home later that he'd made some crack about Marvin's success that Marvin quite accurately didn't take to be simply congratulatory. It was after that that Marvin said there'd been some talk around the Department to the effect that most of the applicants for the fellowships for which he knew Carl was an applicant were former political activists. The talk had made someone nervous enough, he said, to order clearance investigations for all the favored applicants. Whether these would be routine or more assiduous he wasn't sure. They could presumably go either way in any case, depending on what turned up when they started looking. Marvin apparently claimed that he had little to do with the fellowship program, though he knew about it, and nothing to do with the investigations. At the same time though, Carl thought, despite this disclaimer of authority or influence, he was also warning him, telling him not to get too uppity or he'd regret it."

"And Carl then figured he was in hazard and got upset?" Ben asked.

Sarah smiled ambiguously. "You've put your finger on the question anyway," she said. "He was sure he was in hazard, but whether or not that upset him is a lot less clear to me."

"Oh?"

The unrevealing smile persisted as she said, "You didn't know Marvin made a play for me when I was sixteen, did you?"

"The son-of-a-bitch!" he said.

"I was pretty sure you didn't," she said. "Nothing happened though. Even young as I was, I wasn't flattered. I thought he was gross, and let him know that I did. But however much that simplified things then, it complicates them now. Complicates them further, that is. And even without that, the situation would be rich in possibilities. It's only because Carl really could be in trouble I suppose that Marvin can needle him this way. Because he does have a vulnerable past. I don't unfortunately think, given my own history with Marvin, that I'd get anywhere asking him about it, but I'd sure like to know what's actually going on. Marvin might well want to make things look as bad as he can, maybe a little bit because of me, but mostly because he's pissed-off at Carl in a way that's old history both painfully revived and amplified. Carl though may be quite willing to have them look bad too."

"Why that?" Ben asked, remembering that Faith had told him something about Sarah's suspicions in this regard.

"Can't you guess?" she asked, and now she was no longer smiling. "Some part of him wants to be unaccommodatable into the system, or wants that anyway more than it wants to be accommodated. So it's not enough that the real circumstances are poor. I also have to figure out whether it's only circumstances that are working against me, or whether Carl's cooperating with those circumstances in order not to let them wither."

"How about my going to see Marvin and trying to find out what's really up?" he said.

"You're amazing, Dad," she said. "You really seem to believe in the notion my profession professes—that there's a remedy for any injury or potential injury. In this case though, it's hard to know what's actually been done, which makes the issue of remedy very complicated."

"I know," he said. "But it would be no big deal for me to try to find out, and it might just be useful."

"It might indeed," she said. "But it's also likely to be an unpleasant experience. Marvin after all is holding all the trump cards. If he wants to cause trouble, he can."

"I guess," he said, but by then he could feel his body on its way even though he too was sure that seeing Marvin was going to be unpleasant.

5

LUCKY HAD shown little interest in what Faith reported about Marvin Traglich, and was no more interested when Ben told her what Sarah had added to this. She did say that it was generous of him to volunteer to talk to Marvin, but even this was said without much enthusiasm. She obviously didn't think what was amiss between Carl and Sarah lent itself to intervention. For the second time within a comparatively few minutes, he'd run head-on into her stern convictions about the limited possibilities of help—convictions that had only been reinforced by her years of work in a helping profession.

He'd known at once when she returned from meeting on Sunday, and sat behind the wheel in rigid silence while he helped Faith out of the car, that something was amiss. But he didn't know what it was until after he'd settled Faith in her apartment again, and Lucky had returned the car to the garage. Then she told him that her mother had kept lapsing out at meeting. "I've never seen her like this before," she said. "She couldn't have known where she was more than half the time. And it didn't just happen during the silent intervals either. When someone was saying something she could be perfectly attentive for a while, and then be gone in the middle of a sentence."

"Should we try to find out what's happening, or has happened?" he'd asked, knowing even before he finished asking it that the question was a mistake.

"Absolutely not," Lucky said. "I promised when she came out of the hospital after her hip operation that there'd be nothing like that again. All I want for her now is that she be allowed to die quietly at home when she's ready to."

Ben had no alternative wish for Faith, but he had real doubts about the manageability of what Lucky envisaged as the appropriate way for her mother to die—which he knew, though it was never quite said, meant not just how she was to die, but also that this not occur until after they'd had a chance to observe her eighty-fifth birthday the following month appropriately. He didn't share Lucky's confidence in the commanding force of appropriateness. He thought it appropriate to do whatever he could now to help Carl and Sarah, but he didn't think the appropriateness of what he did would necessarily make it effective.

If Carl's clearance ran into trouble, the trouble would be his record as a political activist during the war in Vietnam. He'd taken a leading part in at least one anti-war demonstration considerably wilder than the one in which Ben had first become aware of him, and he'd eventually spent a couple of years in Canada as a landed immigrant. He hadn't been a draft evader exactly because it hadn't come to that. But he'd dropped out of public health school to go to work as a health aide for the Canadian Department of Indian Affairs because he thought he'd be drafted otherwise and have to do something he absolutely didn't want to do as soon as he got his master's degree. His worst possible scenario—and because it was the worst it had struck him as the most likely—was that he'd be assigned to the rural pacification program.

It was obvious enough, in retrospect, that there'd been something quixotic about the way he'd dropped out of school and gone to Canada. Both were symbolic acts, and their symbolic resonance had been a lot more certain than their practical importance. He could probably have taken his degree and still found some way not to be drafted. He might have taken a job with the U.S. Bureau of Indian Affairs which would have had no more to do with the war than did the job he'd taken in Canada. And with his degree, he'd have had some choice of jobs by now that paid well and kept him in one place most of the time. He wouldn't have been applying for a fellowship now, more than a decade later, to make that choice possible. But at the time, Carl's decision hadn't really appeared quixotic to Ben, and though he hadn't encouraged him to do what he'd done—he'd have considered that presumptuous—he hadn't pressed any second or cautionary thoughts on him either. He'd really had none. He'd had plenty of second thoughts since however, particularly once Carl and Sarah had started to live together. From time to time he'd confided some of his misgivings about all this to Charlie Coleman, and it was Charlie who'd then found out about the public health fellowship program. He'd given the information about it to Ben, and Ben had passed it on to Carl. Only he hadn't just passed it on to him. He'd urged it on him. Carl hadn't been much interested at first, but he'd finally had to admit that the program had unique attractions, and he'd applied. And it did have unique attractions. A few selected applicants with appropriate field experience were to be given generous stipends and two years of training to qualify them to direct regional public health programs. That might well take care of Carl and Sarah's problem if Carl saw that problem as Sarah saw it. Or as Ben was most inclined to see it. As a need for greater stability. It had never been clear however, as Lucky had taken care to point out, that a stable life in this sense was the life Carl envisaged for himself. Not consistently anyway. Because it was the only life Ben could envisage for Carl and Sarah together though, he wanted them to have that better chance for it anyway that the fellowship would afford, and it caused him a lot of uneasiness to remember the many conversations he'd had with Carl back when he was thinking of dropping out of school and going to Canada, about how to do this with least burning of bridges. He could see that the efficacy of their joint judgment was about to be given a severe test.

There was good reason not to talk to Lucky about this right now, but he wasn't being entirely forthcoming with Sarah either. For whatever his disposition to seek Marvin out, he too had cause not to relish seeing him. After his last encounter with Marvin five years back, this meeting was going to be a case of having his chickens come home to roost. And Marvin was unlikely to let him forget that.

Marvin had been one of a number of students to whom he'd given jobs at the Phoenix over the years. Of these though, he was the most memorable. He'd been far and away the most useful, and he'd stayed on longer than any of the others. A sophomore when he started, he'd worked part-time during the school year and full-time summers through the summer after his senior year. It wasn't just the length of time he'd stayed with the job though that had made him so useful, nor even that he was very smart. Most of the students who'd worked in the store had been more than smart enough. What distinguished him was an indefatigable ambition to succeed that was a lot less common in the late sixties and early seventies than it had been earlier or had become again since. Marvin had set himself to learn the business as if he meant to take it over. That was the way Ben had set himself to learn it twenty-five years before, but that was also what he'd intended to do, whereas Marvin must have known that once he left college, he'd never be in a bookstore again except as a customer. Probably though he knew no other way to do anything. He collected success the way other people collected stamps or miniature bottles. And he did this with an appearance of bland ease that both was and wasn't mere semblance.

He must have collected more admissions to graduate school and more fat fellowships than anyone else in his senior class, and Ben had written letters of recommendation for each application. Or versions anyway of the same letter. It was a distinct advantage, Marvin had told him, to have at least one non-academic backer. Respectful, intelligent, accomplished, Marvin was the consummate over-achiever, and keeping tally on him became a heady diversion for Ben. Marvin was offered every fellowship and admission to graduate school he recommended him for that year, and after a lapse of three years, during which Ben heard from him occasionally but didn't see him, he turned up again wanting one more letter of recommendation. Ben didn't write that letter however. He advised Marvin confidently and emphatically instead not to make the career change he was contemplating.

Before the conclusion of that meeting, he'd begun to suspect that the view of the nature and limits of Marvin's talents on which his advice was based was faulty. Only by the time these doubts came to focus it was too late. Marvin had come to see him at home, on an August Sunday morning, and though the heat was murderous, he was wearing a dark two-piece business suit with a dazzling polyester sheen. That was probably a common enough style of summer wear then in many parts of the working world, but it wasn't common at all in the part in which Ben worked, and he'd have done well to take this as a first hint that he wasn't on known ground. He'd asked Marvin when he arrived if he didn't want to take off his jacket, and Marvin had thanked him but said that he was fine. He really didn't seem to notice the heat, which suggested that he had the thermal system of a lizard. But in addition he seemed to take satisfaction from the way he was dressed, from not having to pretend any longer to be a boy, and Ben had slowly recognized what he'd certainly been aware of but not quite recognized at the time, which was how uncomfortable Marvin had been in the last stages of being a boy. What had appeared to be a kind of equanimity, must have required unrelenting effort to manage discomfort. Marvin must have felt in perpetual masquerade in jeans and a shirt and sweater, the male students' uniform of the day. Both a uniform and a time into which he couldn't quite fit.

Somewhere along the way though, before that last time Ben had seen him, Marvin had put the trials of pubescence behind him and leaped gladly into premature middle age. In his senior year in college he'd been editor-in-chief of both the literary magazine and a magazine of news and comment that he'd helped found, he'd won two prestigious undergraduate prizes and been awarded a summa degree, and he'd chosen from among all the graduate fellowships clamoring for his acceptance a particularly fat one from the Committee on Social Thought at the University of Chicago that would allow him to bridge disciplines. He wanted, he said, to work around in the intersecting areas of political theory and classical philosophy which would allow him also to go on using his "beloved Greek."

Ben had judged him to be unstoppably launched on a scholarly career, but when he turned up again that summer after four years in Chicago, he was still under full sail but looking toward different seas. He'd come increasingly to believe, he said, that if he was going to spend his life studying political philosophy, he should have some firsthand knowledge of political process. The previous winter therefore, he'd applied for—and predictably been awarded—a summer internship that had just had him in Washington for a couple of months working for the House Banking Committee, and this had changed all his plans. He was crazy about what he'd been doing that summer.

Marvin had always been too studied to be a very convincing enthusiast. He professed enthusiasms, but his professions were always considered. Nothing ever swept him away. He did seem surprised by his enthusiasm for the House Banking Committee, but Ben figured that this was either wishful or specious. Scholarship and teaching could induce in even the most apparently hard-headed academic a yen for the world of action and power, and there were plenty of professors who cherished their stints in the O.S.S. or the Bomb Survey during World War II, or a stretch later with A.I.D., as the best times of their lives. The craving that motored these forays was generally sufficient for only a short run however before they returned to safety. And Marvin seemed a born academic, the prototypical Jewish boy-scholar. He might manage a brief detour—apparently he just had—but he didn't seem cut out for a sustained career in politics or public life. As a consequence, when Ben thought Marvin was asking him what he should do, he told him to go back to Chicago and complete his dissertation.

It had taken him a while to understand that Marvin wasn't asking whether he should move out of the sea of contemplation into the ocean of contention. He was only asking his former employer whether he'd like to help him effect that move as he'd helped him make other moves in the past. By the time Ben realized this though, he realized too that it made little difference to Marvin's confidence in either his decision or his power to implement it to be told that it was a mistake. He'd made up his mind, and he knew plenty of other people by then who'd be willing to write letters for him most of whom had a lot more clout than someone who'd done nothing but run a few moderately successful bookstores in a university town and several nearby suburbs. It could only have been some surprising residual sentiment that had made him turn to Ben this time in the first place.

The following fall Marvin worked as a speech writer for a Democratic candidate for Congress in northern Illinois, and when his man was elected, he followed him to Washington. Ben heard that he was there, but he heard no particulars and soon lost track of him. He'd imagined him from time to time since however, moving up in the complex networks of appointive office. Not in the civil service which would have been too slow for him, but not in elective office either. No electorate was going to commit itself to that bland face with its unfailingly intelligent eyes magnified behind rimless glasses, or that reasonable and controlled but higher than expected voice. Ben could picture him as a guest on the MacNeil/Lehrer show giving expert testimony on some complicated tax matter. Or as someone to lend power to the powers he was entirely probable too. Not however as a campaigner, though he did have his own kind of presence. On his way out of the house after that last interview, as they shook hands, he'd said, "Thank you for all the past help you've given me."

Friendly, precise, and valedictory, this ackowledgment had left Ben feeling unexpectedly bereft. Only now, despite that definitive farewell, they were going to meet again. According to Sarah, Marvin had a position of considerable authority in the U.S. Department of Education. He was based in Washington still, but he spent a number of days each month in Boston, in an office in the J.F.K. Building, and when Ben had phoned the Department early Monday morning, he'd been switched around a couple of times after he'd asked for Marvin Traglich, and then a woman's voice said "Federal Programs."

The voice wasn't federal at all. It was local, from Dorchester probably, and reassuringly friendly. Mr. Traglich wasn't in, the woman said, but he did work in this office from time to time. When Ben said that he'd like to see him the next time he was there, she said, "You're in luck, dear. His calendar says he's going to be here tomorrow and the next day. Is it business or something personal you want to see him about?"

"Some mixture of the two," he said, gambling on her friend-liness.

"Okay. He's got an opening at ten forty-five tomorrow morning. How's that for availability?"

He said it was beautiful, and she told him where to come and added that he'd drawn a lucky hour since at that time of morning he wouldn't have to fight his way onto the Green Line the way she had to do twice each day during the morning and evening rush hours. She was so affable that Ben had to caution himself not to make too much of it. He expected Marvin to be affable too, but that would only be veneer. He'd be dealing with a steely Marvin of whom he'd never been sufficiently aware until their last meeting.

When he told Lucky Monday evening that he'd been able to make an appointment to see Marvin the next morning, she said it was good he could do it so quickly. But when she left for work the next morning without even alluding to how he'd be spending the next few hours, he figured that what he'd told her had either dropped out of her mind overnight, or been pushed out by her more pressing concerns. He spent most of the next half hour then, until it was time to take off himself, wandering deliberately back and forth between the living-room in the front of the apartment and the kitchen in the back thinking about just what it was he hoped to learn from Marvin and how best to go about learning it. Meanwhile though, he was also inspecting the rooms to see whether anything was not as it should be. This practice had always turned up something that needed attending to in their old house where he'd developed it, but it yielded nothing now in the far smaller, thoroughly refurbished apartment except a conviction of reduced circumstances. The apartment was certainly large enough for them most of the time, and it was several notches up from the house in luxury and state of repair, but the marked reduction in both space and visible history was inescapably melancholy anyway. After a while though, he was no longer inspecting but only wandering, trying to ready himself for this impending visit from which he didn't quite know what to expect except that he wouldn't enjoy it.

He left the apartment around ten, and came out to a cold, cloudless day that could reveal the world in unsettling detail. Even his regular route to the subway station was at moments arrestingly unfamiliar, and when the train came up from underground to cross the bridge to Boston, he saw a number of semi-submerged objects projecting grotesquely from the ice on the river—the scoop of a snow shovel, the bottoms of two large white plastic tubs, one leg of a pair of striped overalls, the handle and hood of a wicker pram. When he came up from underground again then at Government Center, on foot, the monoliths rising from the vast brick plaza looked all but inaccessible in the washed air. Much of the plaza itself was coated with nearly invisible ice, and he shuffled his feet to discover where there was and wasn't traction and watched a bent old woman off to his right progressing even more cautiously toward the winged entrance of City Hall, feeling her way with a four-footed cane like Faith's in one hand and a ski pole in the other. She had considerably less distance to go than he did however, and had soon passed out of view.

He was walking into the teeth of a gale. The bite of the wind made his scalp feel as though it was being excised from his head. Of the few people on the plaza, the only ones who didn't seem daunted by the wind and cold were a boy and a girl too young to be here legally on a school day who were sliding across the ice with their arms spread, holding their jackets like sails. The situation wasn't really that extraordinary however. The wind came off the harbor at this velocity frequently. Cooling in summer, though even then there was likely to be more of it than required, in winter it was regularly a hazardous torment.

All of the buildings around him—with the exception of City Hall which was handsome in some inflated, uncivil fashion—struck Ben as ugly. But the J.F.K. Building toward which he was heading took pride of place for sheer inexorable ugliness. Ultimate proof that repetition did nothing to relieve the banality of a banal module, its ugliness was too positive to be attributed to simple misjudgment. It had to be ugliness of intention. He'd had occasion to enter the building only once before, shortly after its completion, when his federal tax return was being audited. He'd come in mid-morning then also, to see Mr. Roger Meagher of the I.R.S. A quarter of an hour early for his appointment, he remembered coming out of an elevator onto an expanse of open floor thronged with desks but all but empty of people. The one person he could find, a receptionist, told him that everyone else was on coffee break and would be gone for another five or ten minutes still. The huge space—probably thirty or forty feet by seventy-five—was articulated only by ranks of steel desks and desk chairs strung along both its axes. And everything else he'd seen inside the building had been similarly provisional. Only the steel and glass exterior looked definitive.

Delayed by the ice, he wasn't early this time but had to wait anyway. The secretary with whom he'd made his appointment—a cheerful matronly woman with curled orange hair and soft wrinkled cheeks that had powder lodged in the wrinkles—remembered him, said Mr. Traglich was making a long-distance call, and asked him to take a seat in the corridor beyond the railed-off area in which she worked with three other women. Tan metal panels behind them screened a series of offices that were only nominally private. Ben could hear voices beyond this wall, and the secretary's voice as she talked to him was carefully subdued. "I actually don't know why he can't get off the phone," she said. "I buzzed him, so he knows you're here, and he's only talking to some pal in Washington he could just call back a little later. The Lord knows what they have to talk about so much anyway. They were bumping shoulders in the same office yesterday and probably will be again tomorrow afternoon."

Conspiratorially concerned about his comfort, she gave him a copy of *U.S. News and World Report* to read and clucked periodically as the voice that he too was soon able to distinguish from the other voices floating out from behind the panels talked, stopped, talked, stopped again, talked once more. He picked up only a word here and there, but the unctuous mildness of the voice which soon sounded as familiar to him as if he too had last heard it only the previous day, never suggested incertitude.

Sitting on one of several plastic chairs just outside the dividing rail waiting for Marvin to finish, Ben experienced a sudden absence of all capacity for desire. In somewhat milder forms, this was not unfamiliar. A conviction that there was nothing he didn't already possess that he wanted. He sometimes thought he'd be happy to discover or even just imagine something he didn't have or hadn't once had that he wanted badly even if he saw little chance of getting it. But there was absolutely nothing on this floor of the J.F.K. Building that he could even think of wanting, and most of what he saw, smelled, felt, or heard was repellent. Smelled most immediately. The odor that the warmth of his buttocks volatilized from the plastic on which they rested reminded him of the floral deodorants he always found more offensive than the known and explicable human odors they were supposed to mask.

Discounting physical objects though, was there anything else to be sought for here? Anything that would justify this talk with Marvin Traglich that he knew he'd be better without if there weren't? He was finding it hard now to believe that there could be. On the ground floor—when he arrived and was getting his bearings—he'd come on a rack of free pamphlets one of which had immediately drawn his eye. Book size but slim, it had a yellow paper cover with a line drawing on it of an attractive young mother, father, and child. A happy American family at first glance, but the title of the pamphlet was "My Child Is a Dwarf," and when he took the top pamphlet from the stack to look at it more closely, he could see that no matter how much this family resembled all the other happy one-child families of fiction and advertising, they were different. The child's tousled head was too large for his body, and though the parents were smiling they were also oppressively pensive.

He'd slipped the pamphlet into his pocket to have a further look at it later, and he took it out now and began to read it inside the pages of *U.S. News and World Report* which he'd turned through very quickly without finding anything that engaged his attention. The pamphlet however was astonishing. Published by the Little People of America Foundation in Owatonna, Minnesota, it was a series of answers to parents' questions, and these lucid little essays were at once exemplary and heart-withering. His own children had all been healthy, and they'd grown up too with no more he supposed than expectable pain, though even that had caused him and Lucky grief that had been keen enough at times. They'd experienced this for Mark particularly, whose life was moving wonderfully now though it still seemed awfully solitary, but who had had a couple of years when he was eighteen and nineteen of being utterly stopped. Years, it seemed to Ben in retrospect, that his younger son had spent mostly in bed alone. Days had gone by when Mark never really got out of bed. And most of that time he and Lucky could do nothing but hang onto the hope that something would change. Which, happily, it did— suddenly and inexplicably. It had seemed at the time—and still did—that Mark had simply decided at a certain point to come back to life.

But some part of Ben also found the pamphlet painfully hilarious. Why? Was it the lucidity itself? While he was trying to understand this better however, reading for the second time the answer to the question "Why do I feel so numb, so angry, so sad?", the voice that had been intermittent background to his reading was suddenly closer and louder. "Ben!" it said, and then more temperately, "Ben Morrison, what a pleasure to see you again. And looking so well."

Ben raised his eyes and closed "My Child Is a Dwarf" inside *U.S. News and World Report*. "You too," he said.

Though his response had been automatic, it contained an element of truth. Marvin did look well. He'd obviously prospered since their last meeting, and had assimilated the gravity of his flesh. He was a man of dignified appearance now instead of a plump boy. How old was he? Not much more than thirty, but the comfort he'd just been coming into five years before was achieved. Though it was winter this time, he wasn't wearing a jacket, and his turtle-neck jersey declared both a new confident sense of himself and the material aspect of his prosperity. The shirt was cashmere, and when Ben took the hand offered him over the rail—Marvin hadn't come around the rail to greet him—it too felt at once soft and durable. Its pressure was friendly, but not excessively so, and Marvin's large clear gray eyes were crinkled in frank interrogation as he waited to be told the purpose of this visit.

Following him back into his office, and recognizing the characteristic non-athletic vigor with which he moved, the decisive up and down that accompanied forward motion, Ben was pretty sure that the only way to proceed was to be direct. To say, if not exactly why, at least about what he'd come. Marvin was far too smart after all not to have made some shrewd guesses about this already. And once they were inside the office that was furnished with the chaste impersonality of a motel, Marvin also promoted directness. "I did some catching up on you when I met Carl and Sarah at a party a couple of weeks ago," he said. "They told me you'd just sold the Phoenix."

"That's right," Ben said, "though it's taking me a while to understand that that's what I've done."

"I can believe it," Marvin said.

His posture as he leaned toward Ben—his hands together on the desk top, palm to palm, the fingers of each clasped over the back of the other—was insistently inquiring now. Seated behind the desk, he had his back to the one large window in the room while Ben, across from him, had the pale but intense ocean light full on his face. "You've made some changes yourself since I saw you last," he said.

"Things have been working out pretty well for me," Marvin said.

His tone said that things were working out better than pretty well, and this transparent self-satisfaction was also familiar. A lot of the energy that fed Marvin's successes had always come from the open pleasure he took in being successful. Success and pleasure in success fed each other in true symbiosis. "If you're wondering what's brought me to see you," Ben said, "I think it might be called not minding my own business."

"I doubt that I'd call it that," Marvin said promptly.

"Perhaps not," Ben said, "but it's essentially accurate none-theless. Apparently you told Carl when you met him that all the favored applicants for those public health fellowships one of which he's hoping for have to get through some kind of security clearance, and that piece of news has made big waves in my prospective family."

"I'm astonished," Marvin said, wide-eyed, his face a perfect semblance of astonishment. "What's the problem? Surely not Carl's now ancient record as a student activist."

"I don't know exactly," Ben said, "but I wouldn't rule that out."

"That's ridiculous," Marvin said, his voice breaking excit-edly as he leaned still further across his desk toward Ben for emphasis. "Not many people in Washington are geniuses, but there aren't many cretins either. And you'd have to be a cretin not to allow anyone who was growing up in the 60's and early 70's some years of smoking dope and a certain number of anti-Vietnam demonstrations the way kids of an earlier generation were allowed to break a few windows on Halloween. How would I be where I am if that weren't the case? Not even the time Carl spent in Canada or his little essays at, if you'll pardon the expression, guerrilla theatre, are likely to raise many eye-brows. They're not such a big deal. He must still be taking himself too seriously if he's upset by what I told him."

"That may be," Ben said. "But it's a great help to my own peace of mind to know that you think he has nothing to worry about."

He said this to move things ahead, and it did. Marvin straightened up in his chair, increasing the distance between them, and dropped his hands into his lap. Then his face dropped too. The animated jolliness was gone suddenly, and he was all business. "If we're to be realistic, let's be as realistic as possible," he said. "I'm certainly inclined to think Carl has nothing to worry about. If he is worried therefore, it's more likely than not prideful worry. But I'd have to add that I never knew Carl very well, so there may be something in his past that I know nothing about that could turn up now and count against him. The government isn't all-forgiving. Let's say it's generally tolerant but that it's not absolutely blithe."

Marvin regarded him as he said this with a distinct edge of chill. "Do you have any possibility in mind?" Ben asked.

"Not really. It would have to have been something humongously stupid, that's for sure, and Carl's not stupid. But that could just possibly be the point as well. If there was anything like that, the grand stupidity of it might have been just the appeal it had for him. You know, what made it look like another form of distinction. He could have figured that he'd surpassed all the rest of us so many times already in all the prescribed modes of distinction, that the only other challenge was to surpass us also in imaginative stupidity. Show that he had the balls to do something really dumb. If he actually did do something like that—and I'd still say that it's unlikely, but nonetheless the attraction it could have had for him becomes increasingly apparent to me as I think about it—then he could be in trouble. You might sound him out about what it is that is worrying him. If you're really curious about those waves you talked about, that is. And let me know if you find out anything."

"All right," Ben said, and was calculating how quickly he could terminate this conversation without his haste being either suspicious or discourteous. Marvin must have something in mind, he thought, but he couldn't be sure what it was, and he decided not to say why it would be difficult to question Carl about anything right now.

6

HE KNEW BETTER than to start this kind of conversation in bed, but he did it nonetheless with remarkable frequency and had the chance then to wonder in the course of the predictably bad night that followed how he could be such a persistently poor learner. It had been especially dim this time though, when what had set him off was his still unresolved sense of the remark Faith had made to him earlier in the day about gratification. On the other hand, he knew why that remark that was also an exhortation had been clanging at him right then. Odd that the idea of gratification could still take on such plangency as he watched the wife to whom he'd been married for going on four decades slide out of her white cotton underwear into a worn flannel nightgown that hung from her shoulders like a sack. Lucky had always scorned provocative intimate apparel. Unnecessary she said if the systems were in good order, and only confusing if they weren't. But he'd felt the systems going inexorably out of order as soon as he began to talk and Lucky turned her head toward him on her pillow and let the book she was reading fall forward, slowly and still open, on her chest.

The day was framed now by bed. That was the frame of every day, of course, but today each of the habitual activities of beginning and ending was marked by an intrusive event—

Annie Ryerson's phone call as they were getting up in the morning, and his attempt now to get Lucky to respond more fully than she'd been disposed to earlier to his reported exchange with Faith at lunch. He hadn't been surprised to have Faith ask him a pressing question—or really two insidiously related pressing questions. A combination of instinct, absence of what sometimes passed for courtesy but was really inhibition, and avid curiosity had always made her a telling interrogator. For as long as he'd known her she'd had this discomforting ability to ask openly just what you were secretly asking yourself. Her questioning was generally kindly however, and today, at first anyway, it had had an edge that made what she asked not quite what he'd been asking himself. Close, but different.

What she'd said was: "Tell me what you think you've been doing recently."

It was spoken casually enough, but it would have been a lot more amiable to ask simply what he was doing. She knew he'd just spent the morning in the Public Library, and to ask what he thought he was doing had to suggest some discrepancy between his sense of himself as he read at a numbered place in the old main reading room and the way he might have looked to someone who saw him there. Or even, apparently, to someone who imagined him there. His self-image was problematic enough. He wondered how much he did or didn't resemble the other men and women, as distinguished from the younger students, who worked in this same room. There were never many, but it was impossible for him not to be curious why any of them were here. To know what allowed or caused an adult to spend the better part of a day—and in the case of the men and women he recognized as regulars here, day after day—all but chained to a library table, reading and taking notes.

The annex was another matter. The large addition joined somewhat arbitrarily to the back of the old building was frequented by casual readers, by drifters and bag ladies who came to warm themselves and use the lavatories, and by the old or otherwise lonely seeking to break the tedium of the day. The population was always comfortably diverse, and included office workers on lunch break in the middle of the day and in the afternoon when the school day was over high school kids. Ben could imagine some hypothetical account for anyone he saw here, but the population of the main reading room over in the old building was more opaque.

The physical contrast between the two buildings was both extreme and emblematic. The annex was a rational cube of bright space furnished with blond wood tables and chairs in convenient groupings. Above all cheerful, it seemed to quite consciously avoid the solemnity of its predecessor. The original entrance to the old library, facing the front of Trinity Church across Copley Square, was kept closed and locked now, and the only access to it was by way of the annex. To get to the old reading room, Ben traversed a long corridor that led from the brightness of the new lobby to progressively interior space until he passed through a heavy door into a cloistered court that had a covered walkway around a dour arrangement of shrubs, grass, and potted plants open to the sky and crisscrossed by gravel paths. At no time had he ever found more than two or three people in the court, though it was quite comfortably warm on sunny days. The lobby of the old library was just beyond this walled-off space for contemplation, and it too was always nearly empty. With its high bronze and glass doors onto the Square sealed and dusty, it looked almost abandoned, but disuse didn't diminish its grandeur. From the hall, he'd mount one or the other side of a double stairway toward a splendidly vacuous Puvis de Chavannes mural under the steady surveillance of two crouching stone lions, feeling something of the astonishment the nineteenth-century explorer of the Yucatan he'd been reading about, John Stephens, felt on coming into the empty splendors of Uxmal, that this had been here all this time and he'd been so little conscious of its existence.

The air of grand historical solitude however, which persisted too upstairs in the reading room—a barrel-vaulted double-apsed nave extending right across the long front of the building—aggravated the sense he had anyway that what he was doing these days was peculiar. At no time when he'd been here had the number of users in this cathedral for study exceeded two dozen, and in the early morning there were sometimes as few as five or six. He frequently sat alone at a table that had designated places for ten readers. He rejected the thought that what he did here had to justify a portion of the cost of keeping the place going, but he was glad that there were only one or two attendants at the desk at which he submitted his request slips, and no more than two or three gophers to fetch books from the stacks. His strangest time here though had been the half hour he'd spent the first day he'd come, waiting at his designated place for the single book he'd requested to be delivered to him. Now he always carried something with him to read while he was waiting, but this was still when he was most aware of the other regular users he'd come to recognize. They were all well-dressed and they all read with unflagging attention, but each also had some distinguishing habits. There were three with whose behavior he'd become particularly familiar. One was an elderly man who always wore a green visor and read in his shirt sleeves and who went to the men's room at least once an hour walking slowly and stiff-legged as an old horse, with his remarkably long black shoes flexing against the floor as though they had no feet inside them but were simply attached to his ankles. Another was an Indian woman of indeterminate age, her eyes emphatically kohled, who adjusted and readjusted her sari as she read, alternately exposing and re-covering a full, rounded, dusky shoulder. And the third was a man who always wore three-piece suits and looked more like a salesman than an academic, who read oversized books in Russian and made notes as he read in a ledger with a leather spine and leather corners.

Each of these was presumably a scholar, but what did that actually mean? And why were they working here? They all seemed to regard themselves as in this room on some recognized basis, which was more than he could say of himself. He wondered what the attendants made of the books for which he'd been asking. On the same day he might request John Stephens' *Incidents of Travel in Yucatan*, Stendhal's *The Life of Henri Brulard*, and a volume of the Time-Life history of World War II. There was a logic to the combination, but it was very private, and sometimes his conviction that he wasn't a true parishioner in this cathedral of inquiry became so distractingly uncomfortable that he'd get up, extinguish his light, and either go out for a cup of coffee or linger awhile in the annex where he figured he had no less right to be than anyone else. Some of the books he was reading were always there too, and on an open shelf so that no one had to fetch them for him. But he really preferred reading in the old library among the pros for whom reading was presumably a form of doing and not mere recreation.

He did want to lead a more contemplative life for a time, recapture a capacity he'd once had that the success of the Phoenix had shaved away ruthlessly over the past thirty-five years even though it had had a lot to do with his going into the book business in the first place. He'd hoped in the free months ahead of him until he started working at Huntington to enjoy having leisure again to read and think. A simple enough ambition. But he had constitutional troubles with it he hadn't anticipated which could make it hard for him to say just what he was doing. Or even what he thought he was doing. Sometimes it felt only provisional or preparatory, and he was too old to be preparing for life.

Probably having to watch him make lunch for her today had been the immediate cause of Faith's asperity, but her question had been entirely cogent. He might very well not have been making her lunch in fact if his uncertainties about what he'd otherwise have been doing hadn't made the prospect of not doing it for a while, and for a useful reason, attractive. Annie Ryerson had called just after seven that morning to say that one of her kids was sick and she wouldn't be able to come in. Faith had seemed a little less well to her the past couple of days though, she said—nothing alarming, but her pulse had been less regular—and she didn't think it would be wise just to let her fend for herself for the day. She also hesitated however to send a substitute, because she wasn't sure Faith would take well to someone she didn't know. Lucky agreed that she was unlikely to and said that she could cover the situation herself for a day. But as soon as she'd hung up the phone, she said, "Oh damn! I forgot. It's no problem for me to stay here into the middle of the morning to get her bathed and dressed, but I'm supposed to be having lunch with my supervisees today."

Ben grunted, and she said impatiently, "What?" She'd come out of the bathroom to answer the phone wrapped in a bath towel and floating vapors of toothpaste and bathwater into the cold air while he was still in bed. This was generally the order in which they got up in the morning, since she woke energetically all at once and he had to persuade himself back to life.

"I can give Faith lunch," he said. "In my new privileged existence, I could happily take off an hour or two for lunch every day if I knew what to do with it."

"You make it sound harder than work," she said.

This time his grunt was part assent to what she said, but part appreciation too of the clean line of her shoulders still above the bath towel. He really was content though to know that the day would now be articulated—that there'd be something he had to do and didn't have to invent. He got up rapidly, and was in the library early enough to be ready for a break anyway by the time he had to return home.

Lucky had told him she'd have the makings of lunch ready for him, and when he arrived at Faith's apartment he found the table set for two and a can of consomme, a couple of hamburger patties, and lettuce for a salad on the kitchen counter. That was more lunch than he generally ate, but lunch was Faith's only meal. A couple of other times in the course of the day she'd make tea or coffee for herself, with toast or biscuits and perhaps some cheese or fruit, but that was the extent of what she could manage alone and she didn't take easily to being helped. Only the regularity of Annie Ryerson's visits, and that Annie was paid for what she did, made even this arrangement relatively tolerable for her.

"Coming back here to fix lunch for me must put a nice hole in your day," she said as he began to do the simple cooking.

He told her it was lunch for him too, and company, and also, as he had Lucky, that he welcomed the interruption, but this didn't help much. "Really!" she said.

While he was heating the soup, broiling the hamburgers, and dressing the salad, she looked at the newspaper. She didn't turn any pages however, and he thought she wasn't actually reading. More likely, encased in the wing-back chair looking toward her lap, she was considering what she was going to say next. Once as he watched her though, her eyes closed, and when her mouth opened then, her face softened and a sequence of small movements passed across it that suggested some kind of distress. It was lapses like this that disturbed Lucky, and he could understand why. But this one was relatively undramatic, and when she opened her eyes again after what couldn't have been more than a minute and was probably less, she was immediately alert.

It wasn't until they were actually eating that she asked him suddenly what he thought he was doing. He confessed that he didn't know exactly, but then didn't leave it at that. "Day by day though," he said, "I'm nosing my way into some books I've been wanting to read anyway but haven't previously had time for. Some of this reading may eventually go into a couple of courses I plan to teach at Huntington. Beyond that it's an act of faith."

Again she didn't respond at once but attended this time to her lunch. Eating was a complex activity for her now that required concentration. After a while however she blotted her lips carefully with her napkin and said, "You're enjoying doing this some part of the time though aren't you, dear?"

"Some part of the time," he said. "When the strangeness of it isn't excessive."

"I'm glad," she said.

His answer hadn't however assuaged her curiosity. "You know," she said, "when I think about my life now, which is most of what little I can do, the times I find hardest to be reconciled to are those that I see could really have been more gratifying than they were."

It was that shift from asperity to benevolent concern that had made the conversation telling. The logic of it was clear. Having asked him what he thought he was up to and received an uncertain answer, it made perfect sense to want him to think about whether his life was as gratifying as it could be. Perfect sense, but also troubling sense. But the abruptness of her shift in tone was troubling in a different way, as was too the finality of her statement with its implied question. Each had to reflect her own understanding of how little energy she could summon any longer for sustained exchange.

Faith had been even more provisionally present once more than she'd been just the day before or the day before that. But she was also disturbed in a way he hadn't seen before. Rattled, or edgy. She didn't like the idea that he'd interrupted what he was doing to attend to her, and he'd only exacerbated the situation by telling her that he welcomed the change. It was no comfort to her to know that he didn't have his life very well worked out right now, though that hadn't been quite what he'd intended to tell her. But he wondered too whether her own circumstances couldn't be made a little less ungratifying.

He'd been trying therefore, after they'd gone to bed, to get Lucky to give more attention to this possibility than she'd been prepared to give earlier. She wasn't at all happy about either her mother's health or her state of mind, but she had a more determined view than he did of what could or couldn't, should or shouldn't be done for her, and it was this that he wanted her to reconsider. In addition to choosing a poor time for this conversation though, he'd started it without much tact. "Are you sure nothing can be done to make things somewhat better for her now?" he asked.

Lucky let the book fall forward very slowly onto the quilt bound tight across her chest by the weight of her arms before she said, "Sarah's right. There is something marvelous about the way you preserve your belief that there's a remedy for any ill. It's marvelous beyond understanding."

"Come on, give me a break," he said. "I don't think there's a remedy for wearing out. But that doesn't mean she couldn't possibly be made less miserable than she seemed to be today either."

"Don't make it more complicated than it is already," she said. "We only have certain choices, and any choice we take is going to have its own set of potential bad consequences, some of which are certain to be realized. I've made the choice I'm least unhappy with because I think it's her choice too."

"Okay," he said, "but what was her talk about gratification today about? It was too pointed to be about nothing. And our lives now might be more gratifying too if we had some informed reassurance anyway—some more knowledgeable judgment than we or even Annie can make—that whatever can be done for her is being done. Thinking that doesn't make me a wimp either."

He'd expected some rise of anger or irritation, and was surprised when it didn't come. "Sure," Lucky said, "it would be great to have a doctor tell us every couple of days that we were doing everything that could be done. It would make things a lot easier. Easier anyway until, so we could be doubly sure and doubly at ease, he'd want to do a few tests. And then, to clarify the information provided by the tests, he'd want her to go in for a CT scan. And then he'd discover something that might be treatable if she could just tolerate being in the hospital for a couple of days. Only a couple of days, unless of course complications developed. She was only supposed to be in the hospital a couple of days remember when they pinned her hip. I wasn't sure we'd ever get her out of the hospital alive though that time, and I know she wasn't sure she'd ever get out alive either. Of course I'd like to have some authority figure to keep telling me I was doing everything right. It would make me feel a lot better than I do feel a lot of the time—and I know I'd be a lot nicer to live with. Only it wouldn't work."

They'd been lying on their backs, in reading posture still though neither of them was going to do any more reading, and Lucky turned on her side toward him now though she was careful not to touch him. "There's something I never told you," she said. "Something that happened the day they pinned Faith's hip. I couldn't bear to talk about it then, and I didn't think there was much point in talking about it later but I can see now that I should have done it."

As soon as she turned toward him, he'd been aware of her body's heat that would have spread through his body as viscous warmth if he'd just slid across the space between them until her head was on his left shoulder instead of being supported on her own right palm. But that wasn't going to happen. "The operation was scheduled, you probably remember, for shortly after noon," she was saying, "and I was allowed to spend the morning in Faith's room even though visiting hours didn't begin officially until mid-afternoon. That wasn't exactly a special privilege. Faith found being in the hospital an indignity and wasn't a very cooperative patient, and so the nurses liked to have me as an intermediary. I got there in time to help her wash up, and then I read and talked to her until the anaesthesiologist came and gave her a shot. The shot was only supposed to make her drowsy, but she must have been weaker than they knew, because a quarter of an hour after she got it she was asleep. Sitting with her then, watching her sleep flat out on her back, I was acutely aware of how little of her there was under the sheet, how little flesh or even skin covered the high fine bones of her forehead, nose, and cheeks, and how faintly she was breathing.

"I probably sat and watched her that way thirty or forty minutes, convinced that she was dying and determined not to summon anybody, to let her go without intervention. I could almost have been happy to let her go this way, because she seemed to be doing it painlessly and easily. Only it shouldn't have been happening there, disguised by the subterfuge of cure, under cover of anaesthesia—as though she were incapable of facing, understanding, even having some deciding power over what was happening to her.

"And then suddenly two black men in green scrub suits appeared in the room pushing a stretcher on wheels. In the confined space of the four-bed room, the stretcher rang against various other pieces of metal furniture before they could get it drawn up alongside Faith's bed, and they were talking to each other as they pushed and pulled it in a language of which I couldn't understand a single word but that I assumed was some kind of creole. I don't think the nurse who'd come into the room with them, presumably to supervise what they were doing, could understand them very well either, but they had a paper on a clipboard that looked like a complicated shipping ticket against which they checked the name band on Faith's wrist. Then they lifted the top sheet from her bed, uncovering her body which the hospital dickey left largely exposed, one poor thin naked leg akimbo and the other in a rudimentary splint. They lifted her onto the stretcher in the bottom sheet, re-covered her and bound her there, and wheeled her out of the room.

"I knew they were taking her to the operating room, but because they looked as though they had to be taking her to some other less mundane place, I followed them. I really had to know at least whether the elevator they'd roll the stretcher onto would be going up or down. In the hall, their skin glowed purple in the fluorescent light, and they talked to each other continuously in deep, sonorous, really quite beautiful voices, and made no attempt to talk quietly—maybe because they knew no one could understand what they were saying. It seemed to confirm my apprehension of what was happening when the elevator they took went down, not up."

Lucky shifted onto her back again now, so that she wasn't talking toward him any longer but toward the ceiling. "I determined right then," she said, "that if I ever got Faith home again, there'd never be another such occasion. I'd been as ready to see her die as I could ever be, but I wasn't ready to see her handled as a consignment to some unknown destination. She had after all always gone out at least half way to meet things. She didn't just suffer her life, not even after she was invalided. Unless prevented from it somehow, she'd undoubtedly go out to meet the end of her life too when she was ready. And frail as she was now, I thought she could probably die whenever she wished. But she'd talked to me about wanting to live until her eighty-fifth birthday and having everyone come to be with her for it.

"She's continued to talk about her birthday quite a lot recently, when she quite notably hasn't been talking about anything further in the future than that—not anyway with reference to herself. She's always tried to live in her own way, and it would have been cruelly wrong for her to be shipped off by those two underworld functionaries in their green scrub suits speaking a language she couldn't have understood even if she'd been conscious. Letting her die the way she'd like to now that that may be possible once more has to be my chief concern. If I blow it again—and I thought I had blown it in the hospital—there'll be no further chances. But I don't think I can not blow it without some cost of which I'm as sure as I can be that Faith is prepared to pay her part."

7

147 KINNOCK STREET was a modest, three story, pumpkin-colored frame house, but the deck of toxic green pressure-treated wood that jutted over most of a small side garden and the black metal storm sash and matching push-out skylights in the lower slope of the roof indicated recent state-of-the-art upgrading. Several adjacent houses had undergone similar transformation, making the block a discrete enclave. Discrete, but not unique, and this recognition brought on another of the ludic flashes that had punctuated his consciousness with more than usual frequency the past couple of days. The neighborhood declared itself to be not for kids or students exactly, but for a next stage of wonderfully protracted American youth. All these houses declared one way or another that they belonged to men and women far enough along on the road to success to have discovered the pleasure of spreading money around visibly, and he just as visibly didn't belong here even if his hair was still entirely black and his body could still move with determined vigor. But here he was, making his way to a rendezvous with a woman half his age. Or if not exactly a rendezvous, the appointment unsettled him nonetheless in ways with which he hadn't been familiar for a very long time. He might even, he thought, project some aura of the illicit, and though he didn't see anyone watching him, he felt under surveillance.

Ludic flashes. The article in *Psychology Today* in which he'd come across the term a couple of months ago had been thin gruel. He could no longer even really remember what it had been about. But he'd adopted the term as a generic label for certain sudden, almost photographic perceptions he had of himself as comic, at play in some unlikely fashion. He'd had a number of these flashes today, all related to the prospect of this appointment with Carl's ex-girlfriend. He'd just about concluded that nothing more could be done about Carl's fellowship until Carl himself got back from Guatemala when he met Lisa in the Coffee Shak and had to think about this again. Carl had a number of ex-girlfriends, a track record in fact that didn't at all recommend him as a son-in-law. He'd been living with Lisa though when Ben first met him, and in Ben's mind she occupied a privileged place among the several ex-girlfriends he'd known since. He'd apparently either not seen her or not recognized her however on a recent previous occasion when, she told him, she'd seen him here.

A quarter of an hour at the Coffee Shak had become pretty well programmed into Ben's visits to the library. After reading for two or three hours, he needed some diversion, and the Coffee Shak was the readiest source of small diversion at hand—a chance not just to drink a cup of coffee which he could generally have done without, but to change environments. He'd turned restless enough after a while in the reading room on this particular morning for the red-tiled tower of Trinity Church, when he found himself gazing through the high windows at it across Copley Square, to look as exotically enticing as one of the domes of San Marco. But when he walked out of the library then, the cold, stony, inhospitable square itself was all but empty even of pigeons and the only place he could think of to go was neither Florian's nor Harry's Bar, but once more the Coffee Shak.

He'd never before encountered anyone to talk to at the

Coffee Shak, but there were always people to watch, faces to study. Face-watching wasn't a new interest for him either. For years now, he'd found it a lot more interesting on average than he found television, but he was pursuing it these days not only more assiduously than usual, but also more selectively. A disproportionate number of the faces that held his attention, he discovered, were the faces of women still too young to have foreclosed any possibilities.

What was this highly selective voyeurism about? A veteran of marriage verging toward old age, to what end was he staring obsessively this way at girls? If he'd really been appraising possibility, he'd have had an eye out for women of a certain age and disposition, but the one time he'd tried that a few years back—during another of the recurrent spells when he and Lucky were having trouble reaching over the divide—had been a conclusively monumental flop. Not exactly a controlled experiment, but it had convinced him nonetheless of something he all but knew in advance—that he had neither talent nor real appetite for philandering. The selective staring he was doing now though seemed intended only to remind him of what it had once been like to feel vividly in the midst of life. With remarkable frequency, the faces he singled out would jolt back his memory of Lucky when he'd first known her. Since he'd never felt very dependably in the midst of life before then, that was a defined moment. And this principle of selectivity might also explain why, on some recent previous occasion, he'd failed to notice Lisa. Though she was only half his age, she was ten years older than Lucky had been at the moment he was bent on recovering.

This time though, he'd been aware as soon as he came into the restaurant that a woman at a table in the back of the room, beyond the counters, was watching him inquiringly. He'd also known at once who she was, and when he began to make his way toward her, she stood up, removed a blue backpack from the other seat at the table to make room for him, and hung it over the parka already draped on the back of her own chair. He'd forgotten how small Lisa was. When she shook his hand, which she did very firmly, she had to lean back to look up at him. But he was half a foot shorter than Carl, and he did remember that Lisa and Carl together, both in plaid flannel shirts and jeans, had looked a bit like Mutt and Jeff. He sensed now though that no matter how diminutive, she was in very good physical shape and was also very determined. She began to smile as he approached her, and her lips drew back from the surprisingly thick white teeth that they'd barely covered even when her face was in repose. Her most striking feature though was her middling blond hair which had the full-bodied tensile lift of a chow's ruff.

"I saw you here once last week too," she said, "but I didn't say anything because I wasn't sure you'd particularly want to talk to me."

"I must just have been asleep," he said.

"Okay, good," she said. "I just got here myself. I haven't even ordered yet. And there's something I'd like to tell you."

A waitress had come then to take their orders, and he'd asked for regular coffee and she for a cup of tea with neither cream nor lemon. He guessed that she was not just fit but into physical fitness, which was suggested too by the erect carriage of her spare torso, clad now in a sweatshirt instead of one of the flannel shirts he remembered. She was also disproportionately long-waisted, so that when they were seated, her eyes, which he'd looked down into when they were standing, were nearly level with his eyes. Pale blue and protuberant, they declared unabashed candor. "It's about Carl that I wanted to talk to you," she said. "He and I haven't been in touch for a long time, but I assume that you must see something of him, since I know he's living with your daughter."

"They've been living together for quite a while," Ben said,

and didn't realize until he saw her smile again that he probably had been telling her that Carl had changed his ways.

"You know, I actually wish him only the best—or almost only anyway," Lisa said. "But that wasn't exactly what I wanted to talk to you about, though it's related. I can't remember whether you ever knew Marvin Traglich."

"The answer is yes," he said. "I just saw him for the first time in years however a few days ago—about Carl in fact."

"Really?" she said. "Why was that?"

Ben had hesitated only for an instant before telling her what the meeting had been about. His account was pretty complete, except that he said nothing about the complicating troubles between Carl and Sarah, and he repeated verbatim Marvin's problematic assurance that Carl had nothing to worry about unless he'd done something "humongously stupid." Something that he, Marvin, didn't know about.

"That's what he was trying to find out about when he took me to dinner," Lisa said.

"Oh?" Ben said. "When was that?"

"Wednesday evening."

"He didn't waste any time. I'd only seen him the previous day. What did he say exactly?"

He thought she must not have heard his question, until he realized why she was surveying the customers at the adjacent tables—a young black man in a U.P.S. uniform working his way rapidly through two glasses of milk and two cream doughnuts, a teen-age couple with red and green punk-dyed heads, a dropsical old woman in a heavy black coat and white sneakers whom he'd seen that morning in the library who carried her coffee cup to her lips in a wide arc over the shopping bag in her lap. Varied clientele, but they all looked absorbed enough in what they were doing to make it unlikely that they were eavesdropping. "You know, neither Carl nor I was ever very close to Marvin," Lisa said when she'd apparently completed her survey. "Only we weren't close to him in rather different ways." She looked at Ben to be sure that he was following her, and then said, "I don't want to sound coy. If you know Marvin, you probably know that he's a dogged if rather unsuccessful womanizer."

"That's what my daughter's told me," Ben said.

"I'm not surprised," she said. "It's not something peculiar to me that brings it out. I'm only one of many. But whenever I'm not conspicuously involved with someone else, Marvin's sure to appear. He has a nose for unemployment whatever else he doesn't catch onto. There's something so transparent about the way he turns up that I don't even feel bitchy about letting him take me to dinner from time to time. I should also say that it's always a lot better dinner than I'd otherwise be eating."

When Ben said he could understand how she felt, she said, "Really? I'm glad, because it's sometimes more than I do myself. But what the hell! Marvin always looks a lot happier than almost anyone else I know. I don't know whether that's despite or because of his odd disposition."

"He looked ebullient to me when I saw him last week," Ben said.

"That's it," she said. "He must be leading some kind of good life. Which may be why I actually like seeing him."

The black U.P.S. man off her right shoulder had finished his milk and cream doughnuts, and the woman in a mink coat who'd taken his place was looking at them with some interest while she waited for her table to be cleared. However, the noise level in this back part of the room, a kind of non-particular drone, was probably too high anyway he thought for her to hear what they were saying. "Tell me a little more about this most recent dinner you had with our happy friend," he said.

"Well," she said. "It was somewhat different from other

such occasions. Less personal, but more troubling. He didn't ask me any of the questions about myself he usually asks— what I was doing, whether I was dating anyone, that kind of thing. Right off the bat, he asked me whether the name Tonto meant anything to me."

"Tonto?" Ben asked.

"That was the code name for Carl's affinity group when he was into guerrilla theatre stuff in college. I don't know whether other affinity groups had code names, but this one did, and the members were Tonto 1, Tonto 2, Tonto 3, and so on. Carl of course was always Tonto 1. If he's never mentioned it to you, that may be because it's come to embarrass him. I hope it has. It should. When I asked Marvin though how he'd managed to get through childhood without knowing anything about the Lone Ranger, he got more annoyed than I'd ever before known him to show. I guess I was challenging his credentials as a quiz kid as well as being evasive. He said that of course he knew Tonto was the Lone Ranger's Indian friend, but that he was pretty sure Tonto had also been the name of some group of activists we'd known back in college when we were all into that kind of stuff. I said I hadn't ever been into that kind of stuff, and he said he knew that but knew too that Carl had been, so I told him that in that case he ought to look up Carl and talk to him. He didn't of course like that either. He had good reasons, he said, for not wanting to talk to Carl about this—not yet at least—but it was only because he was worried about him that he was asking these questions. He meant to try to prevent him, if necessary, from getting himself into a sticky mess. He was, as you can imagine, very pompous about his intentions. Eventually I had to tell him to fuck off, and then he was in a hot huff. I don't think Marvin has things like that said to him very often. We went our separate ways as soon as we'd finished the expensive dinner he was paying for."

"He didn't say anything about what kind of a mess he wanted to prevent Carl from getting into?" Ben asked.

"No," Lisa said. "He said that was confidential. He just told me I should believe in his sincerity. Believe he was interested only in saving Carl from serious embarrassment if he determined he was risking that."

"But you continued to tell him nothing?"

"You bet. I really don't want to do Carl any harm. Only whether this was actually the best way not to, I'm not now sure. Maybe I should have pretended to tell Marvin what he wanted to know, but told him wrong."

"He'd be hard to lie to efficiently," Ben said.

"You're right," she said. "He's too smart. Only what it is he gets for being so smart isn't anything I yen for myself. There's something I should show you though that I don't have with me. Something that puts some heat on all this. Could you come by my place tomorrow afternoon or the next afternoon after I get off work. The next afternoon would be the better of the two."

She'd assured him that this something, whatever it was— and she'd declined to say anything more about it there or then—would interest him, and he'd agreed to come to her apartment at the time she suggested. He'd been pretty sure coming here this afternoon that what she had to show him was going to be disconcerting as well as interesting. But he was disconcerted by her too. The emanations of the unexpected that he'd kept picking up as they talked at the Coffee Shak had been physical as well as informative. Her lean fluent body had been speaking to him also. When he'd first known Lisa, when she was Carl's girl, she'd seemed knowledgeable beyond her years, as though not much could any longer surprise her. But she seemed younger now, or at least more vulnerable, and yet also bolder.

He carried an accumulated sense of comic displacement with

him therefore as he walked along Kinnock Street and then, at
147, up a short flight of brick steps to ring the bell—the middle
bell in a rank of three—that had Lisa's name over it. When
the door opened, she was standing in a small square entrance-
way with doors off to either side and a stairway behind her,
wearing a sweat suit and Nikes. She always ran when she got
home from work she said, and then turned and ran up the
stairs ahead of him still talking. Six five-minute miles could
clear a lot of bad stuff out of your head she said, and she was
only postponing her run today until after his visit, by which
time he'd probably understand her attachment to this thera-
peutic habit. She had to stretch her short legs to take the steps
two at a time, and he watched the elastic flex of her haunches
under her sweat pants until she'd disappeared around the first
landing. She was waiting for him then, holding the door of
her apartment open, when he reached the third floor. The two
freshly painted rooms beyond the door—a small sitting room
and kitchen under one of the pushout skylights he'd seen from
the street, and beyond it what looked like a still smaller
bedroom—were bright and sparsely furnished.

"I actually thought about calling you last night," she said
after he'd shed his coat. "I was going to tell you to forget about
our visit because I was just about to destroy what I'd meant
to show you. But then I thought what the hell—one day more
isn't very likely to make a critical difference."

"Something more has happened," he said.

"I had an unexpected visitor last evening," she said. "Someone previously unknown to me, who introduced himself as
Agent Ray Donnelly of the F.B.I. He quite correctly showed
me his identification card with his picture on it, but I didn't
even have to look at it to know that he was telling the truth.
He was young, clean-cut, chunky, and alarmingly polite. Only
maybe what I just said, correct, was more accurate. He apol-

ogized for just turning up at my door but said he'd tried to reach me by phone a number of times at different hours of the day and evening without success. That seemed likely enough. I am hard to catch, and I sometimes just let the phone ring when I am here too if I don't want to be bothered. And if he was being that persistent, I didn't see any point in saying this wasn't a good moment. I was also curious about what it was he had to say, and he didn't keep me on tenterhooks. He'd come he said because he hoped I'd tell him anything I knew about a group of students who'd been active in the anti-war movement in the Boston area around 1969, '70, and '71 who'd referred to themselves collectively as Tonto. It was his understanding that I hadn't been part of the group, but that I'd been close to some of them."

"Again!" Ben said.

"Exactly. It's too much of a coincidence to be a coincidence. Mr. Donnelly never mentioned Carl by name. I think because he didn't want to embarrass me. But he wasn't just fishing. It was information about Carl he was after. But I found that reassuring as well as disgusting. The idea of Carl applying for a fellowship at this point in his life had struck me as a little too ordinary for him when you told me about it the other day, but having the Feds in the picture this way made it less ordinary."

"I don't think he'd consider their interest in him particularly flattering," Ben said, but regretted this easy shot when he saw Lisa's face cloud.

"I meant what I told you," she said. "I do mean to wish him only well. I just don't manage that with unfailing success. His bloody singularity can still bug me sometimes. His name as such never came up in the course of my interrogation, but the distinction between ordinary folks and extraordinary folks sure did. Mr. Donnelly told me right away that he had no

interest in how often the members of Tonto joined together
to attend rallies or demonstrations. Everyone had done that
he said, though when I said not everyone he allowed that that
was probably true. What he wanted to know however was
whether Tonto collectively—or any member of the group
individually—had expressed opposition to the war in less ordinary ways. Made any more distinctive statements, or maybe
even done something more striking. He'd heard that there were
some very unusual individuals in this group. That was when
I was absolutely sure he had to be talking about Carl."

"What did you say?"

"I told him that some of the people I'd known in those years
who were most active in their opposition to the war had indeed
been very remarkable." Her face recovered brightness as she
said this.

"And then?" Ben asked.

"Well, then I lied," she said. "A simple matter, except I did
it in rather complicated fashion."

"Oh?" he said. He didn't think she needed encouragement,
but what she'd said deserved response.

"I told him I didn't know anything about Tonto and didn't
think a name like that could indicate anything serious. I hadn't
been much of an activist myself, I said, but I'd been quite
close to some people who were. He almost blushed when I
used the word 'close.' What he wanted least I think was to
have to listen to me make any confessions about my personal
life, and the possibility that I might was a running threat I
was happy to keep in the air. I gave him a very pious line
however. I said that essentially if not in all particulars I'd been
in agreement with my activist friends' ideas about the war,
and in particular with the idea that one was not just allowed
but in good conscience required to do something about it. You
can't imagine how noble a position I took. I told him that since
none of these friends had to my knowledge done anything I

might not also have done under the right circumstances, I could scarcely be expected to say anything more about them. If anything I did say were to be considered incriminating, by implication I'd be incriminating myself. Consequently he'd have to report that I'd in effect chosen to take the Fifth Amendment. Isn't that a pretty complicated subterfuge? Particularly when you consider the number of goofy things Carl and his buddies did back then and dignified as guerrilla theatre that I thought were show-off nonsense at best—and, in the one case at least that I'll come to in a minute, a lot worse."

"That's certainly elaborate," Ben said. "And given as you say the dim view you took of a lot of what must now be at issue, it's also heroic."

"Not really," she said. "I think I ought to be sure you understand something. It wasn't all Carl's fault that he and I couldn't make it together. I was young and stupid. You might be glad to know that, given the place he now occupies in your family."

"I am," Ben said. "But what did agent Donnelly say to your taking the Fifth?"

Lisa's eyebrows rose in amused wonder. "Yes," she said, "what did he say? He was gallant about it. He assured me that if I changed my mind, which he hoped I would, nothing I said would injure me. Nor did he think anyone I cared about—this was the closest he came to mentioning Carl—was likely to be injured as much by anything I could say as they might be by the suspicions roused by my refusal to say anything. When I told him he made the ways of our government sound even stranger than I'd thought they were, he professed not to understand me. But he said he wanted to let me think a bit and would come back again if he might in another week. I said that he could obviously do as he liked, but that I didn't expect to change my mind."

"That's where it was left?" Ben asked.

"That's where it was left. Don't you think I handled this rather well?"

Her voice did an odd trick of thickening as she said this that he now remembered—a sound of deep bodily amusement that shouldn't have been issuable from that spare body and to which it was impossible not to respond bodily. Her eyes too, made bright by their light-collecting protuberance, radiated appetite, and he felt the perturbations of a possibility that he knew to be only theoretical. "You bet," he said.

"Thanks," she said. "But it wasn't just to get credit for my behavior that I wanted you to come up here. Excuse me a moment."

She got up and walked the few steps into the bedroom, but continued to talk. "Instead of getting rid of this immediately after Mr. Donnelly left last night," she said, "I simply buried it in my underwear bag. I figured that even if he searched my apartment today while I was at work, which I doubt very much that he did do, he wouldn't look in there. That's the kind of hunch on which I tend to place great confidence."

She came back then holding a picture postcard in her right hand. "I will of course destroy it as soon as you've had a chance to look at it," she said. "It would be particularly poor I think if one of these cards was found here, and I only had it here anyway because I'd just discovered that it was being distributed for sale—though probably the distribution is pretty selective."

The picture on the card was of a one story asphalt-shingled shed pretty much like hundreds of other sheds in and around Boston. What made it less ordinary though was that it was sheathed in flames and at the center of an odd event or happening. A score or so of defaced human figures were moving excitedly between the shed and the camera, and above the flames, a long sign spanning a pair of overhead doors read

Miller Laboratories Building #4. The faces of the animated figures in the foreground, retreating from the flames, must have been erased on the negative, the emulsion scraped away so that they lost articulation and printed black. The bodies however had been left intact, and they were dancing or capering or simply running in rough concert. Like figures on a Greek frieze, except that instead of chitons and sandals, they were wearing ski parkas or heavy sweaters and either boots or sneakers.

Ben not only remembered the picture, he remembered too where he'd seen it before. It had been on the front page of the *Boston Globe*. Only now it had an addition, something that hadn't appeared in the *Globe*. A legend had been hand-lettered across the lower edge of the picture in squat heavy capitals that suggested Hebrew print. "Next Year in Jerusalem," it read, and it was signed "Tonto 1."

8

HE'D DECIDED to ask Charlie Coleman whether there was any likely usefulness to what his nerves had begun spurring him to attempt as soon as he'd had a chance to absorb the implications of the card Lisa had shown him the previous afternoon. When she saw that he'd recognized the picture on the face of it, she asked him to turn it over, and what he saw then was both conventional and unexpected. The back of the card was divided by a line down the middle, the left half for a message and the right half for an address, and at the top of the message side two lines of type read: Memorable American Monument Series / Feelgood Greeting Cards.

"It's for real, is it, it's not a joke?" he'd asked her, and when she told him that it was unfortunately the real thing, it occurred to him more or less simultaneously that this was bad news and that there had to be something to do about it.

The event was a joke, Lisa had said. The card wasn't, except to the extent that it suggested more than had actually occurred. The fire hadn't burned for five minutes before it was extinguished by one able-bodied black man who worked for Miller Labs and another, ancient, gimp-legged black man who was his assistant. And since the shingles were fire-resistant anyway, all the flames did was char some of them a bit. That the card was now for sale wasn't a joke at all, but it was essentially in the spirit of Carl's intention that this had happened even though his intention had been somewhat more limited. He'd really loved that photograph. He'd been entirely content, she thought, to have the fire last only long enough to be photographed. He was ecstatic when the picture appeared in a number of newspapers across the country the morning after the event, and a couple of weeks later he gave some of his friends copies of it, printed as cards with the legend he'd hand-lettered across it himself, as a New Year's greeting. She didn't know just how many cards he'd made. She and Carl had busted up for good soon after the Miller Labs demonstration and in part because of it. She'd thought the whole thing was phony, a kind of illusory politics, and she'd had no patience either for the state of nerves he'd gotten himself into over it in advance, or for his sense of satisfaction afterward. He'd sent her one of these New Year's greetings though anyway, and she had reason to believe unfortunately that the card he'd sent her was the original for this commercial reproduction they were looking at. Or sort of commercial, she said, correcting herself.

Ben thought she'd had to overcome some initial reluctance to explain this, but once she started she didn't falter. A couple of years after she and Carl had split, she told him, she'd taken up for a short time with a guy named Peter Drew. She'd still been on the rebound from Carl then. That had caused her to make a series of mistakes of which this was only one. She and Drew were badly mismatched. Happily though, that became quickly apparent even to them, and they came apart very soon. Drew, who was an aspiring photographer, was only a kid still, young enough to have had no direct experience of the excitements and confusions of the late sixties and early seventies. But he was also just old enough to feel what he'd missed as a deprivation, and he'd set himself to memorialize, as a kind of recompense, the epoch he hadn't quite been able to live. He was a naive but very sweet kid, she said, and since they'd both known so quickly that they'd made a mistake, splitting hadn't been a very bitter event. They'd managed it with remarkably little recrimination. There'd been absolutely no haggling over possessions, and so when Peter had asked if he could have her copy of the New Year's card, which he regarded as a kind of ikon, she'd given it to him without a second thought. Peter had really worshipped Carl, and in a way that was possible only because he'd never known him except by reputation. She even suspected that his knowledge that she'd once been Carl's girl had been no small part of what had drawn him so mistakenly to her in the first place.

Once started, Lisa told him all this in an open, sensible, sometimes even amused way. Not at all coy, and not obviously rueful either, she'd talked as though the vagaries of her life were as accessible as anyone else's to the judgments of common sense. But Ben had occasionally heard a more complex overtone too in what she was saying that he supposed had its source in the uncomfortable difference between the applicability of common sense after the fact, and its applicability before. Peter Drew as she described him, though not otherwise much like Carl, must now have seemed to her no less than Carl someone to whom she should never have joined her fate, and any considerable discrepancy between what you did and how you then judged what you'd done in matters this close to the quick had to be hard to tolerate.

Similarly, letting Peter Drew have the New Year's card when they stopped living together had undoubtedly seemed both appropriate and unimportant, a small piece of generosity. But when it then had bad consequences, it lent itself at least as readily to other terms of description and judgment. Lisa had just recently moved into the apartment on Kinnock Street, and when she discovered a shop in the neighborhood that sold prints, she'd gone in looking for something to hang on the bare walls she'd just painted and come on a stack of postcard reproductions of Carl's New Year's card. She'd known right off and with a sinking heart, she said, that this had to be Peter's work. It all figured perfectly. The Miller Labs fire was precisely the kind of event he'd have wished to memorialize. And the name of the company she found printed on the back of the card then was the clincher. Feelgood was the title of a novel Peter had admired—a zany account of the adventures of a young white man, one of the hip saints of the movement, who'd spent a year working with a black construction gang in the deep south.

She'd lost track of Drew. She knew only that he was married and had a couple of kids, and that when she'd last heard of him he'd been scraping together a marginal living doing some of this and some of that. She hadn't heard that he'd been producing postcards, but she'd been told that he was still doing some photography. And that he was still living by a recognizable ethos long after that ethos would any longer join you to a company of peers almost any place in the country as soon as you declared yourself. Presumably that was still true, and Feelgood Cards was probably only one of a number of enterprises by which, collectively, he eked out a living of sorts. Or perhaps didn't. But she didn't know where he was, and when she thought of trying to find out, she felt daunted. She couldn't tolerate the idea of looking up Peter's friends to ask about him, and she'd gotten nowhere asking the proprietor of the store where she found and bought one of the cards about the nature or whereabouts of the company that made them. She hadn't been able to tell, she said, whether the grotesquely ugly old man she talked to did or didn't know the answers to her questions, but she quickly realized that no matter what he did or didn't know, he wasn't going to tell her anything. On the other hand, she didn't know what difference it would have made if she had found out anything, since she couldn't see herself talking to Peter about the card anyway.

This declaration brought Ben all but conclusively to the

point at which he assumed she'd hoped he would arrive. Could he, he wondered, find out what she hadn't been able to find out? And if he could, if he was able to discover Peter Drew's whereabouts, was there something next he could profitably attempt as well? Two large questions, but he'd felt his body all but on its way almost before he'd formulated them. The prospect of something active and even possibly useful to do was as inviting as the idea of frictionless space. It certainly couldn't hurt he thought to go to the store where the cards were for sale and see what inquiry there produced. But if he did find out something, that would suggest a more complicated next move of which he wasn't sure he should be the agent. He didn't really want to see himself right now as a kind of monogamous knight whose quest was singularly uncompli- cated by erotic embarrassments. That he rather than Lisa should deal with Peter Drew had a lot less to be said for it logically than that he rather than Sarah should have gone to see Mar- velous Marvin. And the observation with which Lisa con- cluded what she had to tell him had been very broadly summary. "It's odd, isn't it," she said. "If Mr. Donnelly is only, as we both think, Marvin's boy, he doesn't really count. That leaves Carl, Marvin, and Peter as the men to be reckoned with in this little drama. But what do these three diverse men who see nothing of each other have in common? What makes the dynamic?"

She'd laughed, uneasily perhaps but with manifest satis- faction. "Sex may not be the best way to keep the world spinning," she said, "but it does seem to serve."

A cogent view of the world, but one that wouldn't figure at all in the conversation he was now going to have with Charlie. It wasn't in Charlie's line. Ben wanted to touch down though with someone who knew how a different world of affairs worked and was worked. The way he was inclined to proceed had suggested itself to him too instantly for confidence, and Charlie was a dependable source for the kind of knowledgeable and deliberate advice he needed.

Charlie always got to work early, and Ben had called him at his office at eight-thirty, asked when it might be convenient for him to drop by to talk about something, and been told to come right over, "You sound a little more urgent than you're quite allowing," Charlie had said.

"I guess I am," Ben answered, "but this isn't really Huntington business, and it might also take a while."

"No matter," Charlie said. "Huntington is soon going to be your home away from home, so we shouldn't stand on ceremony."

This allusion to a "home away from home" had been sincere too. Flip irony wasn't Charlie's style. But when Ben got off the Green Line and came up from underground just opposite Huntington—the proximity of the station was the closest thing the college could boast to a natural asset—he thought it might take him some time to feel at home here. The single high rise building that housed Huntington, a grim survivor amid the city's new prosperity, might once have provided office space for down-at-the-heel businesses or accommodated a YMCA. It had no look at any event of having ever been associated with prosperity. The high red brick facade, articulated only by identically spaced lines of windows, had absorbed a lot of city grime over the years, and when he pushed through one of the bronze and glass swinging doors that provided access from the street, he was in a comparably dingy lobby. A rank of elevators on one side faced a glass-walled lounge running the entire depth of the building on the other side that had no character but size. Even two Ping-Pong tables, a billiard table, and a snack bar didn't impinge on its yawning emptiness, and the placement of the motley assortment of chairs, couches, and tables with which it was furnished looked entirely arbitrary or accidental. There was no one in the room now but a young man asleep on one of the couches and a uniformed guard seated on a stool at the snack bar reading a newspaper, but a couple of young women dressed and made-up in ways that suggested absolutely no social or functional context—suggested instead that they'd just invented themselves—had preceded Ben into the lobby from the street and he waited with them for the next elevator.

Indeterminate, but heavily scented and apparently unknown to each other, they shared the elevator with Ben when it came and both got off at the third floor. He continued alone then, and when the elevator stopped again at the seventh floor, he came out onto a corridor along which offices were closely clustered. The atmosphere was somewhat strange here too, but it wasn't desolate. The air smelled of coffee, several people shared each of the small offices, the floors were carpeted, and there were pictures on the walls and plants on the windowsills. The receptionist, whom he'd met before and who had a Whitman's Sampler open on her desk, said, "Hello, Ben. Charlie's expecting you. He's alone now, so you can just go on in."

She gestured to her left with her chin, indicating the way to Charlie's office that he in fact remembered, and though he liked her informality, it also occurred to him that he might work here for months before he learned either to know people's last names or to do without them. Everything he passed emanated a kind of comfort that bore Charlie's stamp and that only he, it seemed, wasn't quite easy with. It had taken him a while though he remembered to be easy with Charlie himself, or to suspect how shrewd and informed an intelligence was camouflaged by that bland democratic exterior that wasn't meant to booby-trap the unwary but easily could.

What he'd had to recognize finally however was the conti-

nuity between Charlie's manner and appearance and the kind
of knowledge on which the way his mind worked depended.
When he asked Charlie now whether he'd ever heard of someone named Marvin Traglich, the answer was a usefully informed yes. "Oh sure. I've met him a couple of times and also
heard a fair amount about him from a pal I have who works
in the same office. Seems to be a smart cookie. He has a
reputation though for playing his cards close to his chest while
appropriating power almost imperceptibly. You know, for being
one of those fellows who's so much speedier than most of the
other folks around him that he can add the pieces of their jobs
he takes over to his own and still not even seem rushed. He'll
be someone to watch if he doesn't get going too fast too soon
and fall on his face. I imagine there are already a certain number of people just waiting for that to happen. I get the idea
that he's not universally loved."

Ben then summarized what had happened since Carl had
decided to apply for one of the fellowships Charlie had told
them about, reporting what Marvin had told him, the complications Lisa had introduced into the picture, and enough of
Carl's past history that Charlie hadn't known about before to
indicate why there might be real problems. And having heard
him out with attention, Charlie said he was sure that for the
kind of low level clearance that was the only kind even possibly
appropriate in Carl's case, the F.B.I. wouldn't ordinarily do
more than search their files to see if they contained anything
prejudicial. Mostly by now that would just be computer work.
If they were doing more this time therefore, it almost had to
mean they were being prodded by someone. And the prodder
could very well be Marvin if he had some old score to settle
with Carl. But the comforting thing to remember, he added,
was what a poor track record the F.B.I. had with political
suspects. Even in the most flagrant instances, they'd been

remarkably ineffectual, probably because their regular informants were mostly crooks or ex-crooks who naturally knew more about other crooks than they did about oddball dissidents. "There have after all been ex-weatherpeople high on the most-wanted list," he said, "who've lived in New York City or Chicago or L.A. for years, in nice neighborhoods, doing their shopping in the supermarket, taking in movies and concerts and going to P.T.A. meetings, who finally had to give themselves up when they got tired of waiting for the feds to find them."

When he turned though from general expectation to Ben's instinctive plan, he was a little more cautionary. He was sure it made sense to try to get the postcards out of continuing circulation. The more copies there were around the more likely they were to rouse unwanted attention. Unfortunately however, it was also quite possible that they'd done that already. And particularly given this possibility—that he might be trying to close the stable door after the horse had already escaped— Ben would probably do well to proceed with caution. Hard to say of course just what that might mean. But the store where Lisa had found the cards could be under surveillance—and, if Ben managed to find Peter Drew, he'd better consider the possibility that Drew was now under surveillance too. He'd just have to balance one risk against another as he went along.

The way Charlie applied himself to this matter had to be indicative of how he applied himself to the running of Huntington. There were always facts to know, personalities to take account of, probabilities to be calculated—and when each of these considerations had been allowed its comparative weight, better and worse ways to proceed. He'd been at work when Ben arrived, at his desk in shirtsleeves in his small, hot, rather tacky office, tie loosened and collar open and his seamed, pudgy, somewhat oversized face shiny with concentration. He moved out from behind the desk to talk though, and they'd conferred side by side on a maroon Naugahyde couch that occupied most of one wall. He'd carried the telephone from the desk and placed it on the floor next to him and every few minutes his secretary would buzz him about something and he'd scoop up the phone, listen to her, then either make a quick decision or tell her he'd have to get back to her later. While he was on the phone, Ben would look at the framed panoramic photograph on the wall opposite the couch of Charlie, his wife Ramona, and their five kids—all in summer shirts and shorts or slacks—standing next to a big shiny aluminum camper against a background of snow-covered peaks that could have been the Teton Range.

He knew why the idea of working at Huntington had seemed an opportunity to him, but he knew too that this could have its deluded aspect. Charlie was an American phenomenon. He couldn't have happened anywhere else. But he didn't happen here as frequently as the mythology suggested. It was a lot less than sure therefore that his happy fit with Huntington suggested comparable possibility for anyone else, and Ben could only wonder whether things would work out well for him here as he thought how nice it would be if they did. When it was settled between them that whatever the hazards, it was probably better for him to proceed vigilantly as he was inclined to than to do nothing at all about the Feelgood postcard, Charlie turned toward Ben on the couch—his comparatively large head moving more freely than his small, soft, surprisingly delicate body—and indicated that their conference was really concluded. "Some pair of public servants we're going to make," he said. "Here we are on company time conspiring to keep the wool pulled over the government's eyes—if, that is, that's still a possibility."

9

AS SOON AS HE arrived at the print shop, went in, and saw that the figure blissed out on a splay-footed, cracked leather couch next to a wood stove in the back of the room, wired to a Walkman, had to be one of the twin brothers Lisa had told him about, the character of his mid-afternoon stroll changed abruptly, became immediate. Until then, it had been pretty archeological.

That had just happened though. Initially, he'd set out for the address Lisa had given him to see if he could discover something more about Feelgood Cards and with nothing else in mind. But this began to change as soon as he elected to cut across the Common and the overpass to Cambridge Street instead of taking the more obvious route down Massachusetts Avenue. Once on the overpass, he was virtually on automatic pilot. There were whole stretches where he could have closed his eyes without much risk. He had in fact done that once, years back, after he passed a blind student tapping his way along the path between the Yard and the Science Center with an arduous mixture of caution and determination. Moved by empathetic compulsion, he'd kept his eyes shut for a couple of dozen steps, until he heard someone walking toward him. For just that brief time though what he was doing had seemed entirely possible enough to be awful.

When he turned left off Cambridge Street then, he was no

longer taking an alternate way to Central Square. He was
making an intentional diversion to pass the house he'd lived
in for more than two decades, and familiarity had attendant
hazards. It was almost five years since he and Lucky had moved
to the apartment on the river, and though the changes made
to the house in that time hadn't been many or radical, and
he'd seen most of them before, any difference at all from what
he wished to remember could feel like dispossession. The clap-
boards were painted a glowing barn red now instead of their
former dull brown. The porch, too close to the street to be
usable anyway, had been torn off to make the front yard larger
and let more light into the livingroom. And in the interest of
light too, a three-windowed bay jutted from the wall where
the single livingroom window over the garden had been. He
recognized each of these as an improvement, but that didn't
prevent them from feeling like repudiations. They confused
the memories he'd come here to freshen. He quickly noticed
smaller, more recent, additional changes too. The lilac bushes
next to the driveway had been pruned, and the rickety front
fence had been extensively repaired. These were both jobs
he'd had it in mind to do or have done himself before they'd
moved out, but that he'd never gotten around to. The present
occupants were altogether more conscientious about mainte-
nance than he and Lucky had been in this house they'd occupied long enough to grow into first and then grow out of.
Each slope of that process had been absorbing in its own way
though he remembered. Memory was an all but instant surge.
He didn't have to linger to encourage it, but went by quickly,
eager not to meet any of his former neighbors who still lived
here. He didn't relish the idea of being asked what had brought
him back today or why he didn't come back more frequently.

It hadn't occurred to him though until he backtracked and
was crossing Cambridge Street heading for Broadway that he'd
. also pass close to the apartment Carl had lived in, most of the   .

time with Lisa, the first couple of years he'd known him. He'd only been in that apartment once, and he could no longer remember on which of two or three streets between Broadway and Harvard Street it was located. But though here too as in most of the city there'd been a certain amount of gentrification in recent years, almost nothing had been torn down or replaced, and he readily recognized the drab red brick tenement when he saw it from the corner of Broadway. He really wanted to see the apartment itself again though and not just the building. Or if not exactly see it, see into it. What he remembered particularly was a view he'd had of it once from the street, through a window. He figured he ought to be able to look through that same window again, though what he'd see when he did would at best be only superficial aspects of what he remembered seeing then. That quick view still emblematized for him a kind of incipient adult life he'd never lived himself and frequently wished he had.

Carl had an aversion to heights that he'd only recently overcome sufficiently to allow him to travel by air with no more than tolerable discomfort provided he dosed himself all but comatose with Valium. One of the advantages for him of this apartment had been that it was on the ground floor, though he was more comfortable than in the basement apartment he rented later in the South End. The windows of the apartment were so close to eye level for anyone passing on the street, that Ben had found himself looking into the livingroom once almost without intention. That had happened at night though. He'd been looking from the dark into a lighted room, and in daylight now when he tried to look into what he was certain was the same room, he couldn't see past the frayed and yellowed panels of lace curtain impinging on either side of the window that wouldn't have been there when this had been Carl's apartment.

He crossed the border of scraggly winter lawn between the sidewalk and the building therefore, and by standing on his toes, could just press his nose to the lower edge of the window. He hoped no one would be in the apartment at this time on a weekday afternoon, and he wasn't concerned any longer about being observed by someone on the street. Here anyway it was very unlikely to be someone he knew, and given his age and his respectable appearance, he wasn't likely to arouse much suspicion even if he did look absurd. He was unprepared for the Cairn terrier that bounced up inside the window when his nose touched the glass, but no one was roused by its convulsive wheezing alarm, and after a first involuntary recoil with his heart thumping shamefully, he was able to disregard the ridiculous, wiry, minuscule animal alternately cocked back on tensed legs and springing at the sill, snapping its tiny bright teeth together convulsively. And again, it didn't take much time for him to register what he required. The high-backed Victorian couch against the far wall of the room, the unfinished shelves that supported stereo components and books, the few assorted chairs, and the door on cement blocks that served as a coffee table were all unexpectedly familiar. If not quite the same, they were essentially interchangeable with the furniture Carl and Lisa had had when they lived here.

When he'd seen enough and turned away, he discovered that he had been under observation. An older woman in a black cloth coat with a rather mangy fox collar had stopped on her way into the building—a bag of groceries in one arm, and her other hand holding the door—to watch him. "A friend of mine lived in that apartment years ago," he volunteered blandly. "I was just walking by and had an irresistible urge to see how much the place had changed. Not very good manners, I know."

The woman said nothing, but she continued to watch him

suspiciously as she went into the building, and then waited just inside the door for it to latch properly behind her. And what he'd told her was significantly untrue. He hadn't just been walking by. That was what he'd been doing though on the occasion when he'd looked through that window and seen Carl and Lisa. He hadn't known previously that they lived here, and he'd been arrested by what he saw before he even quite recognized them.

Carl had been pacing the floor of the small room however in a way that had already become familiar to Ben, moving back and forth across it in a rhythm that was purposefully broken for punctuation, and also gesturing vehemently but less regularly with his hands and arms and with sharp thrusts of his head and neck. And Lisa was sitting on the couch, leaning toward him in what looked to be precarious balance. Her mouth was slightly open and her eyes were crinkled, but she wasn't yet laughing. As Carl built to the climax of whatever he was saying, they looked equally rapt, caught up in some complicity to which her audition was as integral as his recitation. Ben had never before seen Carl look so unguarded, which had something to do with his inability to allow himself to watch the performance through to its conclusion.

The one time he'd been in the apartment however, probably a year or so later, had been very different. Carl had been very much alone there then. It had been a Sunday afternoon, a week or so before Christmas and just before the Miller Labs demonstration of which the postcard he was on the trail of now was an amplified record. He hadn't known anything about the demonstration before it took place though. He'd only known that Carl was in a bad state. Bad enough so that he felt he had to go see him even on a Sunday afternoon.

Phil and Mark had both managed to come home early for the holidays that year, and it had been family custom for them to spend Sunday afternoons together when they could, generally doing very little except enjoying the one time in the week when this was possible. He'd been concerned about Carl for some days by then, and if he hadn't known that Phil and Mark were to be at home—if there'd been only Lucky and Sarah—he'd have asked him to join them. Probably for supper. He didn't know whether it was something about Carl or something about his sons that had made him suspect it wouldn't be a good idea this time. That they wouldn't mix well. Probably, he thought, each had contributed to this suspicion he hadn't wanted to test.

After dragging his heels for several hours, he'd finally set out to check on Carl even though he knew how odd his departure would seem to Lucky and the boys and perhaps even to Sarah. Worried about Carl already, his worry had been exacerbated when he tried to call him in the middle of the day and found that his phone had been disconnected. There had been more than sufficient basis for worry too, but he had the basis somewhat skewed. The last time they'd talked, which must have been a week or so earlier, Carl had told him that he and Lisa hadn't been getting along and that she'd decamped and gone to live with some friends in Central Square for a while. Once earlier, he remembered, Carl had confessed that he was just about incapable of living alone, and particularly of sleeping alone. Civilized people didn't sleep alone, he said, and he'd pretty much given up that barbaric practice as soon as he left home to go to college. As soon as he could, that is. He guessed Ben could understand why, he added. That had been only one of several occasions when Carl indicated his assumption that their lives were somehow homologous no matter how grossly different their immediate circumstances of which age was only the most obvious.

The curious thing though was that he'd shared that assumption of spiritual and psychological kinship. And that Sunday, in his comfortable house with Lucky and his three children, his image of Carl alone in a relatively bare student apartment finally goaded him out of the house. It couldn't have been very late yet when he left, but this was the time of the winter solstice, the shortest days of the year, and he'd set out in the most discouraging of early twilights. Nobody was out just to be out. Not many people were out at all, since it was Sunday, and those who were out were pressing to get to where they'd be inside again. One memory he'd never lose was of a similar time in the winter of 1944–45, just before the German counteroffensive, when he'd gone back to Paris for a few days on a special leave, and one late afternoon, with no particular place to go, stood on the bridge near Notre Dame and watched everyone else on the bridge who did have somewhere to go hurry by him.

This mid-December in Cambridge though he'd set out with both somewhere to go and somewhere to return to after he'd been there, and what had compelled him out finally was the understanding that though Carl did literally have somewhere to be, he had insufficient reason to be there. He'd all but discounted the idea that Carl had found someone by then to replace Lisa. The disconnection of the phone was a very bad sign, since ordinarily Carl spent a lot of time on the phone.

And when he got to the apartment, he did find Carl in a terrible state. He'd been so sure in advance though of the cause of the trouble, that he then misconstrued a lot of what Carl actually told him. Carl's indirectness of course reinforced this self-deception. He alluded repeatedly and obsessively to an impending trial or test, but he never mentioned the Miller Labs demonstration as such, sure apparently that Ben knew intuitively that this was what he was alluding to despite the fact that he'd never said anything to him about it. Ben, sure that Lisa's departure was causing Carl's misery, took whatever he said only as further indication of how upset he was. This continuing misunderstanding absolutely depended on their weird working assumption that despite all the obvious differences in their characters and situations they were in some significant fashion kindred souls. And to a far greater extent he imagined than Carl, Ben still retained some version of that conviction.

However wrong his attribution of cause though, his instinct that something was badly amiss had been correct. Even Carl's fastidiousness about his appearance, self-conscious enough at times to suggest that he was dressed for a masquerade, had broken down. He looked now as though he might have been wearing the same flannel shirt and jeans for days, and perhaps slept in them as well. And he'd been all but abjectly glad to see Ben. His capacity for speech, which wasn't generally deficient, had been slow and uncertain at first, as though he hadn't talked to anyone for days, and his lips trembled in anticipation before words issued from them. He might well have been sick, but he was also furtive in a way that wasn't a normal consequence of illness. He didn't that is look as though his flu or pneumonia or whatever it was he'd caught had confined him to his apartment. He looked rather like someone who'd put himself out of circulation. And when Ben said something about his phone being disconnected, he said that he'd simply forgotten to pay the bill.

Empathetic preconception had leaped in though to fill any breach in explanation. Lisa's decamping would of course, Ben thought, make Carl feel both deserted and ashamed. It all made sense. And yet it was remarkable that some more accurate understanding hadn't been arrived at somehow. Carl had after all asked him whether he'd ever known he was going to be tested soon in some way he'd never been before, and waiting for the test to come, wondered from day to day whether he was going to crack under the strain. Had Ben experienced this he wanted to know, and not cracked, and managed finally to do what he absolutely needed to be able to do? Not just made some gesture, so that he could tell himself that no one would be able to say he hadn't tried—or blame him for having fucked up—but done what he had to do as well as he thought he could have done it if he hadn't been in such a bloody funk. If Ben could tell him that there had ever been such a time in his life that he'd come through that way, that would, he promised, make a really tremendous difference to him.

In retrospect it was hard for Ben to understand how he could have continued to be so sure Carl was talking about Lisa's absence and the state in which this had put him. Or for that matter how his response had allowed Carl to think he must know at least the general nature of what did have him under so much strain. He'd talked to Carl at length about what it had been like for him to be in the army for more than three years. He told him that he'd wondered at the end of his very first day in the reception center whether he had it in him to survive another similar day, and that most of the following thousand plus days had each ended with pretty much the same question. But that he believed he'd probably comported himself effectively and honorably nonetheless. If Carl thought Ben knew what was troubling him, that might have been because he didn't understand the role played in all this by Ben's forced separation from Lucky. Though that was a large part of what Ben had been thinking about, he'd been indirect too. He'd allowed himself to be reserved about it, counting as Carl had too on a kind of understanding between them that didn't require everything to be spoken.

One way and another then, the confusion just hadn't been dispelled. Carl had never said: Oh, no, I'm afraid you've misunderstood me. Lisa's decamping isn't what has me in such a

state. She only decamped actually because she had no liking
for what had me in that state already. Instead, he'd thanked
Ben fervently for coming to see him and being willing to talk
to him this way, and said it had probably made a profound
difference in his life. He'd all but panted with gratitude, for
in those days, Carl wore his heart more nearly on his sleeve
than he did any longer. And thinking about this now as he
walked the rest of the way into Central Square, Ben could
even imagine that if it hadn't been for the encouragement he'd
given Carl that day on the basis of this mutually constructed
misunderstanding the culpable postcard might never have existed and he wouldn't have been on his way to this print shop
Lisa had told him about.

The place was called Jake's, she'd said. It had been in existence for a little over a year, and was run by a couple of
outstandingly ugly brothers, identical twins, named not Jake
but Wolfe, but referred to in the neighborhood as Jake One
and Jake Two. Actually, no one seemed to know one from the
other, and it had taken a while for people to realize that there
were two of them. No one she'd talked to had ever seen more
than one of them at a time, but they were known to live
together behind the shop which doubled as the front room
of their apartment. Probably the business was a combined
retirement activity and tax dodge. Both brothers had been
compositors, and they'd been retired with pensions when the
plant where they'd worked for many years stopped printing
from hot metal. But they'd been interested in graphics for a
long time too, and the shop allowed them to make something
of this interest and also write off part of their rent as a business
expense. In a time-honored tradition of printers too, they were
old lefties of some denomination. Their histories were nearly
indistinguishable. They'd always lived together, and they ex-
hibited in extreme form the fleshly exclusivity of a certain class

of old celibate men. They defended themselves against the world, but against women in particular, not just with hostile caution, but with their ugliness as well which was too extreme not to be in part at least cultivated.

Only maybe that wasn't quite right, Lisa had said. Maybe it wasn't choice. Maybe they were repellent because the flesh revenged itself on bodies that allowed it no pleasure. Not only had they decayed, but the decay wasn't regular or consistent. She wasn't sure she'd ever before seen anyone who looked quite so asymmetrical as whichever of the two Jakes it was who neither got up nor faced her either as he said he couldn't tell her what she wanted to know. He'd been slumped sideways on a couch at the back of the store, one shoulder toward her, and he'd regarded her antagonistically from one eye only. A dim eye too, she said. She wondered how much he could actually see.

Whether it was this Jake or the other who was in the shop when Ben found it now, Lisa's description was cogent. The tilt at which he was slumped into the couch suggested some strong indisposition of the flesh to resolve in balanced proportions, and when he unbridled himself from the Walkman and stood up—as he hadn't done for Lisa—the anomalies of his constitution were even more startling. His body was small-boned and must have been fine once, but over time it had taken on sedimentary mass. Mass rather than fat. Lumpy, solid, it adhered to his frame unevenly all the way from the top down. One temple bulged, one jowl was fuller than the other, one shoulder was higher, and he had a spastic mode of locomotion, taking longer steps with his left leg than with his right.

Ben located the postcards at once on the furthermost of the three display tables in the center of the room but decided not to approach them with any hurry, to browse his way toward them instead, looking at what was on the intervening tables and in the bins on the two side walls. His questions might have a better chance of being answered, he thought, if it wasn't obvious that his purpose in coming here had been to ask them. So he turned through a bunch of Daumier reproductions in one bin and some engravings of mid-nineteenth-century Boston in another and looked at the prints of birds and small quadrupeds, some in color and some black and white, on the middle table. He didn't know whether the prices lightly pencilled in the upper right hand corner of each print were reasonable, but few of the prints were cheap. Those of small quadrupeds though seemed to be priced according to the species of creature depicted. Squirrels and rabbits were two or three times as much as rats and mice.

Despite his preliminary caution however, he must have evidenced a different order of interest when he reached the table with the postcards, for Jake—whether Jake One or Jake Two—diminished the space between them at this point, closing on him with that unsettling alternation of longer and shorter steps Ben had noticed when he first got up. If he was as Lisa believed particularly distant with women customers, he didn't exactly crowd Ben either as he watched him examine the cards. They occupied half or a little less of the table, and there weren't many of them altogether—a few Childe Hassam paintings of the Common, some old photos of Scollay Square and the Back Bay, several Copley portraits, and then the card of the Miller Labs fire and another of a rooster mounting a rabbit which was identified as a Feelgood Card too but of a different series called Life in America.

The figure hovering a couple of yards from him broke silence when he picked up the top card on a sizable pile of the Miller Labs cards. "You're looking at the hottest item in the shop," Jake said, "and I don't mean that as a pun. That's the second packet of those cards we've almost run through this week."

The words issued one at a time, measured and distinct enough presumably for even the slowest wit to comprehend. Only it took a distinct and exasperating effort for Ben to listen this slowly, not to forget the last word while he waited for the next. Ostensibly a form of courtesy, this very conscious speech actually felt more like aggression. Hard to know though whether to attribute it to shrewdness or stupidity, a difference that might be critical if he was to find out anything. "That's interesting, that so many people are drawn to that picture," he said, and when after this cautious answer he was asked if he knew what the picture was, he said that he thought he did but wasn't certain.

"The building was part of the old Miller Laboratories," Jake said. "Before Miller built a new place out on Route 128 where not so many people have to be aware of them. Not so many who don't think much of what they're up to anyway. Those smart kids in the picture were trying to burn the place down back in 1970, but unfortunately they couldn't quite get the job done."

"That's what I thought," Ben said, and then added tentatively: "It's one of Peter Drew's cards, isn't it? I know a good friend of his who's talked to me about him. She's eager to get in touch with him as a matter of fact but doesn't know where he is."

The few still expressive portions of Jake's face which had been showing a certain amount of animation, retreated abruptly now into the irregularly larded mass in which they were invested. Even the eyes had shrunk into their fleshy recesses and lost lustre. "Someone comes around every couple of months selling the line," he said. "I don't know his name. We tried a few of their other cards too at first, but this was the only one we could do anything with—this and the dirty one. So now we only stock these two and he doesn't have to spend much time here when he does come around. We don't have much chance consequently to get to know each other."

"I see," Ben said. "And you don't have any idea then where Peter Drew is located?"

"Absolutely not," Jake said. "You're not the first person who's asked either. A few days ago it was a girl, then only a few days before that it was some thug I spotted for a detective. This Peter Drew, if that's who he is, has a very varied bunch of people curious about him, but I wouldn't tell you even if I did know anything about him, which I don't. I figure that if he's producing that card, he's on my side. Just the same as I thought at the time that the kids who tried to torch Miller were on my side."

"Fine," Ben said. "I won't try to explain why I'd like Peter Drew's friend to be able to find him. I can assure you though that it isn't to cause him grief."

"That's as it may be," Jake said.

The vehemence in his voice, or its sound level, must have been unusual, for behind his back at the rear of the shop a thick short-fingered hand pushed aside the curtain in the doorway and Ben found himself looking at something Lisa had said was never seen here—Jake One and Jake Two in whatever order lined up one behind the other, each in a white shirt with an open collar, shiny wool trousers, and black shoes. But it wasn't quite as though two people were staring at him adamantly. It was more like a single reinforced scrutiny. He didn't attempt to extend the conversation, but shifted his attention to a couple of bins of wildflower prints. Before he left the shop though, he returned to the table on which the postcards were displayed, and when he picked up the top Miller Labs card again, to buy this time, he noticed something he'd failed to see before. The packet of cards under it was still unopened, and the return address on the mailing label was The Massingham Printers, Massingham, Conn.

IO

IT WASN'T Sakhalin Island, but it was a place he thought he hadn't known existed when he saw its name printed on the wrapper in Jake's the previous afternoon. And though by morning he was no longer sure of this—overnight, while he slept, some weak association had begun to stir, and now the name Massingham kept teasing at some trace of memory—he knew at least that he'd never been here before.

Last night it had been a surprise too that he was to undertake this expedition with Lucky's blessing. He'd anticipated skepticism and perhaps even opposition. Neither his walk to Jake's in the first place however, nor his return home, had gone quite as he'd expected either. Having walked to Central Square by such an indirect route, he'd decided to return by subway, and the ride that should have taken three minutes had taken three-quarters of an hour. Most of that time though the train had been stuck between stations, waiting for a train in front of it with a fire in its electrical system to be towed off the main track into the yards. He could have walked home in the fresh air in only fifteen or twenty minutes, instead of which he'd had to sit impatiently sniffing burned rubber for twice that time before this complicated emergency operation was completed. He'd figured Lucky was home already, and since these days he was always home when she got there, that she must inevitably be wondering where he was.

About that anyway, his expectations had been correct. The way Lucky looked up at him from the book she'd been reading when he came into the livingroom—she hadn't come into the hall to greet him—was palpably controlled, and he began at once to tell her where he'd been and what he'd discovered. Probably, he thought later, not being able to unburden herself of her news when she got home and he wasn't there was what had made her edgy. But that edge had disappeared quickly, and she was a lot more engaged by the discovery he'd made at Jake's than he'd had any previous reason to believe she would be. She'd endorsed his plan to go to Massingham and agreed that he'd do well to go at once the following morning. It was only too bad the next day was a working day she said after they'd pulled out a map on which they located Massingham, because if it hadn't been she'd have gone with him. She'd never been in that corner where Massachusetts, Rhode Island, and Connecticut came together. No main roads seemed to go through there, and it might be a pleasantly overlooked area. But it didn't make sense to delay his trip until Saturday. If there was anything useful to be done in Massingham, the sooner it was done the better.

His news had displaced hers for a while, but it must also have been what she'd learned that afternoon and not yet told him that had caused this unexpected response. He had no way to know that however for some hours, until after they were in bed and had made love which had also been a surprise. That didn't any longer happen very frequently. He couldn't have said exactly what else about their love-making had changed aside from its frequency, but that change was absolute by now even though it had come about very slowly. Once the nights when they didn't make love had been notable, and now it was notable if they did, and the other changes were far less definite. They didn't admit of quantification, and whatever had happened cumulatively or on average was effectively obscured by the repetition of small fluctuating differences. He was pretty sure though that when they did make love now it happened more slowly—that if the act itself wasn't of longer duration, the affect was certainly prolonged by a certain amount of anxiety in advance complemented by gratitude afterward. And infrequency also placed a significance on each occurrence that Lucky seemed able to accept with an equanimity he couldn't always manage himself. "Not bad for a couple of survivors," she'd said cheerfully when they were once more lying side by side.

"And unexpected as well," he said.

"Not for me."

"I guess I didn't have the possibility in mind," he said. "Maybe because it's been a while."

"And because every time we get out of practice, getting started again seems less likely?"

"To put it optimistically."

"But I am optimistic," she said. "You're the one with the streak of constitutional gloom."

Her fingers moving against his thigh now were reassuring, not tentative as when they'd made their inquiry earlier. The other change he was clear about was the extent to which desire had to originate as thought now rather than as peremptory bodily assertion. But he realized after a moment that Lucky's touch was preparatory this time also. "Now for an interesting sequence," she said. "Sarah wanted to come by this evening to talk to us, but she had a meeting and couldn't, so she phoned me at the office instead and we had lunch together. I was going to tell you about it when you got home, only you had your own big news and I didn't seem to want to follow it right away then with mine. Maybe I was reluctant to upstage you."

"Okay," he said, "what's happened?"

"She's pregnant," Lucky said. "She suspected she was, because she'd been feeling lousy every morning for about a week, and she went out and bought one of those convenient new home pregnancy tests that weren't around when we were concerned with such matters, and confirmed her suspicions."

He heard himself grunt now, as though he'd been squeezed hard around his middle, but all he was conscious of thinking or feeling was that the sequence as Lucky put it really was odd. "Is that why you feel so uncharacteristically protective of Carl suddenly?" he asked.

"Be fair," she said. "I've never been down on Carl except as a potential son-in-law. But I realized talking to Sarah today that pregnant or not, she wouldn't have given him up voluntarily in the near future even if she thought she should. I can understand that, and I also don't want to go on cherishing disappointment. If nothing had changed, she might have been worn down enough eventually to give him up. I don't know that she would, but it's possible. But she might also have been too old by then to have a family with someone else. Should I be wishing for that?"

"But what's going to happen now?" he said. "I don't suppose Carl knows about this."

"Not yet. He's supposed to call her again sometime in the next couple of days, but she's not sure whether she'll tell him when he does. The job in Guatemala is not working out very well, and she may just wait until he gets back before she gives him anything else to be troubled about. She doesn't think he'll be gone more than another week or ten days now, and she's determined to go through with the pregnancy no matter what happens between them. So she says there's no rush for him to know. That could of course be bravado. I'd bet they'll get married when he comes back. I hope anyway that they will. But even so, unless Carl's work life gets a little more conventional, you and I could find ourselves doing some more active child-rearing than we ever expected to be doing again."

"All my muscle for those activities atrophied a couple of

decades ago," he said, "and I don't think there's any way it would regenerate."

"You really are gloomy," Lucky said.

Ben had been lying with his hands behind his head, staring up through the dark at the almost invisible ceiling, and she'd rolled over toward him then so that her head lay in the hollow of his shoulder and one breast was against his chest—defined there for a moment but then losing definition, becoming only a source of soft, increasingly diffused warmth until he was no longer certain where her body ended and his began. "I got to be called Lucky for good reason," she said, "and we've also really lucked out together. Three healthy grown kids. Two grandchildren, and now another coming. No money problems. And we're still not quite decrepit. I could say more, but I don't want to boast. It didn't have to be this way, so let's not be stupid. The gods of fortune can't like ingratitude, and it scares me when you act glum. I want us to have some good times together still even if I am an old woman and don't look or act as though that was on my mind. That's the way I want to look and that's the way I want to act. But I want you to know it's not all I am all the time."

Her rate of speech had been decelerating, and she seemed to go to sleep the instant she finished. After a few minutes though she stirred, and the touch of her breast was again distinct, a defined crawl against his ribs. "I just don't want her life to turn sour," she said, speaking very slowly now, "and I'd a lot rather she didn't have to follow him to some awful place a million miles from here to keep that from happening. I'd like to have some continuity in our lives. With Phil settled for good it seems in California now, we're never going to see much of him or his kids, and even when we do they all, and the kids particularly, seem a little unexpected. Californian I suppose. As for Mark, I don't know whether he'll ever get married and have kids. It keeps seeming more possible all the time, but it doesn't happen. And since I'll be losing Faith soon too, one way and another if things don't work out right for Sarah you could find me getting pretty glum myself."

She rolled over then so that her back was toward him and went to sleep again, and after a while he'd gone to sleep too. But his sleep was disturbed, agitated by dreams he couldn't remember but was in the vague hold of still the next morning when he got up before Lucky for a change, to make a prompt start for Massingham. The sequence of event and revelation in the course of the evening had disturbed a notion of order some vestige of which he retained still from his childhood— that the generations displaced each other decisively. He'd really assumed when he was a kid that there was no simultaneous experience, nothing immediately in common between what was happening to him and what was happening to his parents. An odd idea, but a benevolent one as well. If there were this absolute difference, the generations would regard each other only from a sparing distance. He'd long since known of course that this wasn't true, but it could still unsettle him apparently to experience its untruth.

The drive in the morning, alone in the car, did little to dispel the hangover of the night, and when he'd arrived in Massingham and discovered that he couldn't attempt what he'd come here to do before evening, he set himself consciously, and with some success for a while, to make the most of whatever opportunities for amusement the place afforded. After a late lunch, he walked the main street looking into store windows, then ducked into a movie theatre to see a revival of *Singin' in the Rain*. Along with about twenty other oddly unoccupied people of both sexes and various ages but mostly he thought over fifty, he'd watched Gene Kelly romance with Debbie Reynolds and sometimes dance with Cyd Charisse, and the novelty of doing this in mid-afternoon was even mildly heady. But when he came out into the darkened street again after the movie, he was suddenly assaulted by a combination of headache and existential nausea that he hadn't experienced since he was a boy, going to Saturday afternoon matinees— entering a movie theatre in daylight, and coming out in the dark to a sudden melancholy perception that the day had died while he was gone.

It would still be an hour or so before he could see Peter Drew who went on shift at the Texaco station at seven o'clock. He'd learned this from Drew's wife, who had been remarkably forthright and helpful. Neither her house nor the way she was dressed had prepared him for the somewhat pedantic care with which she explained where and when her husband could be found and why she didn't know where to find him sooner. All the interest of the day had had to do with the circumstances attendant on finding Drew, not with actually finding him which turned out to be no problem at all. Ben had run on The Massingham Printers at once when he arrived, in one corner of a largely disused mill building at the edge of town, on the bank of a small fast river that looked like trout water, and an elderly woman who was alone in the office knew where Drew lived and was happy to tell him how to get there.

A little after noon then, following her instructions, he'd turned off a two-lane county road between a pair of decayed wooden columns on which the white paint hadn't been re- newed for many years. There'd been traces of snow on the ground still almost as soon as he got west of Boston that morn- ing, and here the fields were white and the shoulders of the roads were covered with several inches of hard crust. But the long driveway had been cleared, and the scrub to either side of it was lopped back to two tangled walls that grew together again high over the last stretch to form a tunnel. Beyond the tunnel he came onto open fields with wisps and hummocks of brown and gold stubble showing through the bright white, and the driveway climbed, dipped, then climbed again to a small white house with green trim and a green asphalt roof. Before it quite reached the house though, the plowed lane veered right to a deeply weathered barn from which the doors were missing. The building was open to the elements in other less defined places as well, but it was full of stuff. Lines of jars and bottles on shelves gleamed in the deep, light-streaked gloom of the interior. A yellow Datsun truck jacked up in front of the barn in the posture of a horse taking a fence had had both its front wheels and most of its windows removed. Cannibalized, Ben figured. The whole place was generically familiar.

As he was parking near the truck, a young woman had come out of the house onto the open front porch pulling a ski parka over a heavy sweater. Then as he was walking across the yard, he noticed two children in striped Oshkosh overalls watching him too through the storm door behind her. "I'm looking for Peter Drew," he said when he was close enough to talk.

"He's not at home right now, he's out working," the woman said, and her speech at once fractured the previous coherence of his impressions. Genteel, halting, but precise, it had received its formation in some other kind of life. She could have been one of Sarah's friends, he thought, and wondered whether the chronic depression suggested to him at once by her wan mien had been caused by these changed circumstances or had caused her to seek them out. Their conversation was too brief to tell him much about this though. When he said he'd like to see Drew if he could, that they didn't know each other but had common friends, she was sufficiently reassured by this explanation to volunteer that her husband odd-jobbed all over the place during the day so that she never knew where he could be reached, but that beginning at seven in the evening he worked a half-shift at the Texaco station at the west edge of town. He could always be talked to there, she said. The attraction of the job in fact was that the station did very little business in the evening.

Facing a long afternoon then with little to do, he'd gone back into town and found a diner where he had a BLT and a cup of coffee. The place was pleasantly lively, and there was something reassuring about the familiar mediocrity of the food. As there was too about the local adaptations of the war between the sexes reflected by the signs on the walls behind the counter and between the windows. "Keep your hands off the waitress." "Work for women's liberation; leave your wife." "Our cow is dead but we don't need your bull." The adaptability of the old themes was obviously inexhaustible.

When he returned to the diner after the movie though, its charm had worn thin. His sudden letdown coming out of the theatre and finding the day spent wasn't helped either when he called Lucky. He'd wanted to let her know that he'd be getting back later than he'd anticipated, but this didn't seem to be of much interest to her. Puzzled, he asked whether something was wrong, and she said she couldn't be sure just why, but that Faith was definitely worse. When he asked how, worse in what way, she said she'd told him already that she didn't know. Weaker maybe, she said, but she didn't want to discuss it over the telephone.

The diner had been busy in the middle of the day, but it was almost empty now, and the poorness of the food was more extreme. The fried chicken special might have been Styrofoam, and the look and taste of the pale amber coffee suggested that hot water had been run through the same grounds too many times. By contrast with Lucky's day, he thought—at work, and then coming back to Faith—what he'd been doing was deficient in gravity. In general there was insufficient weight to his existence these days, and even his approaching meeting with Lisa's ex-lover Peter Drew, whom she'd chosen not to see herself, was an arbitrary undertaking from which not much could reasonably be expected.

Nonetheless, here he was, and when he left the diner now, returned to his car, and drove to the Texaco station at the far edge of town where the main street became highway again, he felt a kind of animal anticipation just from being in motion and having an object. He knew he was in the right place when he saw the yellow Datsun truck parked behind the garage. It was the twin of the truck he'd seen earlier jacked-up in front of the Drews' barn, but this one, which had four wheels and all its windows, was the cannibal. He pulled far enough onto the concrete apron before parking not to block access to the tanks. The station was deserted, but the tanks were lighted and there was a light too in the office, and when he'd walked around to the front, he could see a young man wearing steel-framed glasses reading at a desk in the rear of the office. Then his foot hit a hose running across the apron, a bell rang twice, and the man got up and peered through the window. Probably he couldn't see Ben at first but could see that despite the alerting message of the bell no vehicle had drawn up to the tanks, and puzzlement verging on irritation created a band of tension across his long pale face on which his pursed mouth looked both too small and too tender. He was clean-shaven, but his dark hair was long and drawn back severely in a pony tail. In the absence of any other cultivated aspect of appearance, the pony tail seemed emblematic of that loyalty to a past at once recent and distant that Lisa had talked about, and Ben opened the door and said, "Excuse me, are you Peter Drew?"

"Ah, you the fellow who was looking for me earlier up at the house?"

His speech was reluctant, and his only reaction when Ben identified himself as an acquaintance of Lisa's was to say "ah" again. Whatever suspicion or even just plain curiosity this may have expressed seemed a lot weaker than his palpable wish not to be disturbed. But when Ben said he hoped this wasn't a bad moment, Drew assured him that it was fine. He spoke with a slight drawl that sounded invented rather than inherited —Maine and Tennessee in precarious combination—and his manner too was odd. A couple of fingers of his right hand prodded Ben courteously toward a metal chair with a green vinyl seat that stood in front of the desk a few inches from the back wall where quarts of motor oil and gallons of anti-freeze were stored on low shelves with a variety of belts and hoses hung on hooks above them. Before he could sit down again himself though behind the desk, a black Cadillac drove up to the tanks, and the bell issued its peremptory double clang once more. "My boss could turn what's already a pretty good job into a perfect job," he said, "if he'd just make this station self-service after six. I've told him I'd be willing to take a pay cut if he did, but even so the idea doesn't seem to grab him. I shouldn't be but a couple of minutes though."

No one just came to talk, look, and act like that Ben thought as he watched Drew button the sagging, leather-patched tweed jacket he was wearing over a flannel shirt, turn up the collar, and go out to attend to the car. It took invention. The big indoor-outdoor thermometer on the wall next to the window read sixty-six degrees inside and twenty-three outside, and Drew tensed as he hit the difference. Then when he'd placed the nozzle of the hose in the tank and set the catch to automatic, he brought his hands to his mouth and blew into them, shifting stiffly and impatiently meanwhile from foot to foot. He was so self-created Ben decided that there wasn't much more than that fact to be learned from watching him. The only thing to

do now was wait until he returned, then show him the postcard
bought at Jake's and ask him whether Feelgood Cards was his
business. The answer to that was probably anticipatable, so
the question could be no more than an entry. An entry to
what though? If he was going to ask Drew to withdraw the
card from circulation, how could he make that a reasonable
request? Or, even better, have the idea of withdrawing it occur
to Drew himself as it were? As it were? The way Drew comported himself suggested a lot of resistance to subterfuge.

Outside on the lighted service island he stopped blowing on
his hands now, drew the gas nozzle out of the tank of the
Cadillac, hung it up and turned off the pump, then walked to
the driver's window to be paid. He didn't look like someone
who should have been pumping gas, but neither did his appearance offer any clear suggestions as to what he should have
been doing instead. Nor was the copy of W. J. Cash's *The
Mind of the South* lying open and face down on the desk much
of a clue, except perhaps as it accorded with the elective sound
of his speech. The Cadillac was gliding off again, accelerating
rapidly, and Drew was heading back to the office, adding some
bills as he went to a wad he'd taken from his pocket after
raising his right shoulder to make the pocket accessible. Then
he jammed the aggravated wad abruptly back into the pocket,
hurried back to the tanks to retrieve something, and began to
sprint after the Cadillac which was by now only a pair of
receding red tail lights.

Holding something out toward it in one hand as he ran and
shouting for it to stop, he'd gone a hundred feet or so down
the road before he gave up and turned back. The object he'd
held extended toward the car was cupped in his palm now at
waist level, and he was looking at it with his tender mouth
puckered in bemused question. Not until he'd come through
the door into the office again though, could Ben see that he

was holding a cap for a gas tank. "Those poor dumb bastards drove off before I could get it back on," he said, "though the fact is of course that if I hadn't been thinking about something else entirely, if I'd really been doing what I appeared to be doing, I'd have had it back on before I took their bread. It wasn't until I was almost back in here again in the warm where I wanted to be, that I remembered, and by that time they were on their way. Gone. So now when I listen to the eleven o'clock news, I might just hear about a car being incinerated somewhere between here and Hartford."

This account conveyed more pleasure than consternation however, and when Drew slid the bottom drawer of the desk open and dropped the cap into it, he said, "That's seven of the little buggers in there now, all accumulated since October first when I took this job. And yet no repercussions at all— no protests, no one after my ass. If that means I'm providing average acceptable service, you've got to figure the American system is even more fucked-up than anyone is quite suggesting."

The anomalous gleam in Drew's eyes encouraged Ben to declare his business at once. He took the postcard from the inside breast pocket of his jacket, placed it face up on the desk, and said, "Lisa thought you made and distributed these—that Feelgood Cards was probably a one-man operation and you were the man."

Drew only glanced at the card, then picked up a toothpick and clamped it speculatively between his upper and lower right molars. "You interested in buying me out?" he asked.

"That possibility hadn't occurred to me," Ben said, acutely aware of the poverty of ideas that had occurred to him.

"It would be accurate in a couple of ways to call that my hottest item," Drew said, repeating Jake's witticism. "There are apparently a lot more people around these days than you'd think who are still harboring destructive impulses."

The pressure of his jaw on the toothpick when he finished

talking gave his mouth more definition, but only a semblance of toughness. "That's a complication," Ben said. "I was going to ask you to consider withdrawing it from circulation."

Drew regarded him intently for a moment, but his face revealed little of what he was thinking. Then he said, "You mustn't anyway be working for the F.B.I."

"You could say that was exactly what I'm not doing," Ben said.

Drew removed the toothpick from his mouth and leaned back in the swivel chair. "Maybe you ought to tell me what it is you are up to," he said.

"Sure," Ben said. "It's because I'm afraid that card might really be of interest to the F.B.I. that I'd like to see it disappear. I think it could get someone in trouble."

"Some hypothetical someone, or someone in particular?" Drew asked.

"Someone I have reason to believe you particularly wouldn't want that to happen to," Ben said.

"That's likely right," Drew said, "but I'm also very doubtful about that possibility. Before I started hustling that card, I blew up the original as big as it could go without fading into nothing, and made certain that no one on it could be identified. Whoever it was scratched out the faces on the negative did a very thorough job."

Ben had thought this far himself. "Probably," he said. "But seeing that picture around could irritate some people at least as much as it gratifies others. It might stimulate some very aggressive inquiry, and it's hard to know what would turn up if that occurred."

"You think?" Drew said. "I figured that by now the fellow must be pretty much untouchable. I take it we're not mentioning names."

He nodded understandingly when Ben said he'd just as soon not, and then swung his chair around a quarter turn to face out the window. "Taking that one out of circulation would really take the heart out of Feelgood Cards for me," he said. "I wouldn't have much interest in keeping the business going without it."

Was this the sound of someone getting ready to drive a hard bargain? Ben couldn't be sure, but he thought not. "I didn't realize what a critical item it was for you," he said. "I'm not trying to buy you out, but maybe some compensation for your loss could be arranged if you did agree to withdraw it."

Drew was more quietly amused now than when he'd come back into the office with the gas cap in his hand. "It's not the money, man," he said. "I don't want to shit you. All I make on Feelgood Cards altogether is a tax loss, and last year I didn't have enough income to take advantage of the loss. There'd be no reason to keep the business going at all if I had to stop distributing the picture of the Miller Labs fire, but not because it makes me any money either. It's only that I have a lot of deep feeling for that card. Every time I look at it, it tells me that life could be beautiful. That's what Feelgood Cards was supposed to be about, but the only card in the line that really does it for me is this one. The others—the civil rights marchers, the anti-war rallies, the pretty pictures of cannabis plants that get sold mostly to people who don't smoke any more—they're all pious. Dream stuff really. But that one picture, even if it isn't quite the real thing, gives you an idea of what the real thing might be. You follow me?"

"From a distance," Ben said.

"Yeah, I know," Drew said, and swung back to face Ben across the desk. "I really do know who we're talking about, don't I? You can tell me that much without mentioning any names."

"I'm sure you do," Ben said.

"That's what I was afraid of," Drew said. "I particularly

wouldn't want to risk getting his ass in a sling. He's too beautiful—or was anyway when I knew something about him. You really think I could cause him woe?"

"If that card got into certain hands, it could really mess up his present plans," Ben said. "Plans, incidentally, on which I also set some store."

For a moment, Ben thought the issue was about to be resolved. But then he could see that Drew was still turning something around in his head. "Unless he really has changed though," Drew said, "that picture has to mean at least as much to him as it does to me."

This too Ben had thought about, but he hadn't been able to deal with it. All he could do now therefore was be evasive. "Maybe so," he said, "but does he know someone's been offering copies of it for sale?"

"I couldn't say. I haven't been in touch with him and maybe I should have been. But if he did know, and knew also what a popular and heartening item it was in its own small way, do you think he'd want the fellow who was making those copies to stop making them?"

Ben took a deep breath and held it a moment before he said, "I certainly hope so."

He didn't realize quite how obviously this was a prevarication however until Drew had thanked him for being so up front. "Tell him and ask him," he said. "If he says that's what he wants, I'll destroy the plate and whatever prints I have on hand. That's not all that many, because I can never afford printings much larger than I have orders on hand for. I've got a buddy at the print shop who does these tiddly-shit printings for me as a favor, and out of fellow-feeling. It'd be a sorry day for both of us if we had to stop doing them, so the request will definitely have to come from our unnamed friend."

"Fair enough," Ben said. "Only he's out of the country at

the moment, and I won't be able to ask him until he gets back."

"Okay, I'll declare a moratorium," Drew said. "I'll hold everything for a week or two to give you time. Not much happens in this business in a week or two anyway."

Ben said that was fair enough too. They shook hands then across the desk, and he left after getting Drew's address and phone number. The drive from Boston had taken almost three hours, and since it would probably take somewhat longer going back in the dark he didn't want to linger.

I I

HE'D JUST ABOUT decided he must be wrong—that the conviction that Massingham had once meant something to him had no foundation—when accumulated irritation triggered the connection. Sergeant Riley had come from another Massingham, in New Jersey. He must have heard him talk about the place, but he remembered particularly now seeing the name on the return address of the letters he'd received from Riley in the first months after they'd both become civilians once more.

The drive in the dark on unknown roads—the emptiness hardly broken by his swift passage through small towns that were closed down for the night if not quite blacked-out—had probably helped him remember, jogged him back to that past that wasn't simply distant now, but scarcely seemed any longer even to be on the continuous line of his life. It was an all but self-enclosed blip instead, off to one side of the line. The onset of that discontinuity had compelled him to stop answering Riley's letters. They'd become close friends in the year that began in Normandy and ended in Czechoslovakia even though he was a commissioned officer and Riley was a non-com, but they'd moved so rapidly in very different directions once they were out of the service, that the distance between them was soon too great to bridge. It was hard for him to believe now that they had once been friends. But he couldn't really believe either that he'd actually been in the army for almost four years. Whatever he could still remember about that time might almost have happened to some Ben Morrison of whom he still had strong, dependable, empathetic knowledge, but who was someone else.

That long stretch of time had had its shaping influence on what he'd become though, and in ways that weren't apparent only to him either. Carl had once told him that he'd felt it a deprivation as he was coming of age—something he'd tried to make up for in various ways most of which now struck him as comic or delusory—not to have, as Ben had had at the comparable time in his life, a morally acceptable war to satisfy his appetite for large risking activity undertaken for the common good. He'd been surprised to hear Carl commit himself to such an unironic formulation. But he'd been far less surprised then to hear Mark, whose view of existence was more earnest, talk about this same difference more particularly.

The last two years Mark was in college, he'd worked nights as a security guard at a housing development in Everett where the incidence of assaults and unnatural deaths was at least double the annual average in Greater Boston. As long as his son actually held the job, he'd never asked him why he'd taken it. But when, shortly after he got out of college, Mark announced that he was going to give it up, he did ask him, and asked too why he'd stuck with the job so long. Mark had said he wasn't exactly sure, but that he thought about the time he'd put in there as a partial equivalent for the time Ben had spent in the army during World War II. He'd derived a lot of satisfaction over the past couple of years from the discovery that he could get along with, like, even admire kinds of people he'd never known before and hadn't been sure he could get along with, and it had also been a relief to him to discover that little as he enjoyed being scared, he could tolerate that too. He'd rubbed a thumb knuckle along the bottom of his nose as he said this, a sign that he felt himself getting more serious finally than he was comfortable being. Now that he'd held the job for a while, he could admit that it had begun to bore him, he said, but he could probably also leave it with fair confidence that whatever he'd discovered would be there to fall back on when he needed it. Like money in the bank, he said, to lower the moral tone of their conversation.

Ben knew that his years in the army had deprived him of certain kinds of experience for which he'd never made up, in part at least because he'd been so certain by the time he got out of the army that it was too late. But the other side of that had been an unformulated but operative conviction that his three and a half years of daily misery had been a purgatory to be followed by reward. That if he just lived earnestly, he was likely to have a good life. And, remarkably, this was to a very considerable extent what had happened, only it was often hard for him to believe now that this life he had and valued was an earned life and not just a lucky one.

Mark's reasoning, and Carl's, had had renewed resonance for him recently as he tried to look back into that time again. Carl hadn't however said anything about learning to tolerate fear, maybe because that was something he'd never done, and he was particularly curious about that tolerance. He'd been reading the Time-Life history of the war to try to relate what he remembered of a few days in the spring of 1945 to the larger pattern of the end of the war in Germany. He was pretty sure that the personal significance for him of the assignment that he and Sergeant Riley had shared then was something he hadn't yet altogether fathomed. It was probably remarkable that he hadn't been killed in the course of those few days, which distinguished them significantly from the relatively safe war he'd known most of the time, but he remembered them as passed in a state not of open fear, but of high-minded misery that must in part anyway have been fear's masquerade.

He hadn't exactly volunteered for this assignment, but he'd been ready as usual to attempt whatever was at hand and purported to be necessary. In some respects at least, Carl's formulation had been accurate enough to his own sense of the war then. If not an opportunity exactly, it had created an undeniable, perhaps even insatiable demand for the performance of large, uncomfortable, presumably significant acts for the common good. Reading the Time-Life history of the war though to find out whether any real basis was suggested by the larger picture of what had happened for the potential value he'd attached to what he was doing for those few days had gotten him nowhere. That larger picture was so large that it was virtually abstract, and he could make no connection between it and what he remembered. What he remembered though wasn't very considerable.

He knew however that the signal battalion in which he was a platoon officer had advanced to somewhere east of Kassel. Kassel was one of the relatively few place names from that time that had stuck with him. They were moving toward the Elbe, and the Wehrmacht was rapidly disappearing in front of them—or appearing as lines of disarmed and dispirited soldiers walking west under guard toward improvised prisoner-of-war camps. Almost a year had gone by since the Normandy invasion, and though it had been apparent to him that the character of the war was changing, he hadn't yet understood that it was finally almost over. The corps to which his battalion was assigned was advancing very rapidly though, considerable distances every day, and this was cheering but also created problems. The armored division attached to the corps was advancing so fast that it would recurrently lose all contact with either corps headquarters or any elements of the two infantry divisions supposedly on its flanks. More often than not this happened at night when radio signals faded.

After it had happened three or four times, the corps commander had declared without much attention to natural possibility that there were to be no more such lapses, and the ambitious assistant C.O. of the battalion, a major named Carrington, then came up with a bright idea. Carrington loved to have bright ideas, and this one had set his clipped rufous mustache quivering with pleasure and excitement. If corps would detach a couple of half-tracks to him for security, he proposed to send out a mobile radio team to serve as a relay between the armored division and corps. The team would cruise during the day to maintain good reception from both cp's, and then come in as a relay whenever division and corps were unable to receive each other directly. This brilliant but not necessarily feasible idea was quickly approved, and Ben was designated as leader of the mobile team.

He wasn't the obvious choice for the job. Liccione—a shrunken, bow-legged lieutenant from Newark whose prematurely wizened face looked as if it had had a long soak in formaldehyde—knew a lot more about radios than he did. But Liccione had also grown up street-wise, and made a point of letting it be known that he was timid. Loud noises still scared him he said even after almost a year of having to listen to them, and he'd busied himself assiduously in the repair truck the entire morning the relay proposal was under discussion, keeping his acute nose in among the condensers and vacuum tubes where it did literally seem able to sniff out trouble. Ben meanwhile remained visible and said when asked that of course he'd be willing to take on the job. If he hadn't actually been attracted to the hazard of it, he must at least have thought that he should be and acted as though he were. And the mission must also of course have seemed important to him.

He remembered remarkably little of what had happened in

the course of the next several days except that by monitoring corps and division, and moving around during the day to keep the strongest signal from each but with little sense otherwise of where they were—they'd run off their maps on the second or third day—they did actually succeed in doing what they'd set out so improbably to do. They served as a relay at night when contact between corps and division would otherwise have been lost, and did this until for some reason—probably a tactical decision made at some echelon of command higher than corps—advance in that sector was slowed sufficiently to allow communications to be consolidated. Ben wasn't even sure how long they'd done this. Probably four or five days. He and Sergeant Riley had both eventually been rewarded with bronze stars, but he had no idea whether what they'd done had been of any actual importance.

That whole adventure had been muffled for him by a deadening coexistence of high-minded dedication—he'd entertained at least the possibility that what they were doing could actually speed the end of the war—and a state of animal misery that had to have been caused in part at least by the repression of fear. If he'd been scared keen as he should have been, he might now remember every significant detail of those few days when he'd led a couple of radio vehicles, two half-tracks, and twelve or fifteen men around the German countryside guided eventually only by monitored radio signals that weren't being broadcast for their benefit. They didn't ultimately know more than vaguely where they were, and they had no idea where there might still be pockets of armed German soldiers small enough to be overlooked with impunity by the armored division in its preoccupation with speed, but large enough to raise hell with their little detachment. He'd tried not to let himself think about such possibilities though, and this willed disparity between operative consciousness and gut perception must have induced some mental and emotional paralysis. Interestingly enough, the only event of those days he did recall in any detail had to do with someone else's terror.

They'd come into a village one evening toward sunset when the corps and division signals were beginning to fade. It sounded as though they were about halfway between the two cp's, and he decided that this would be as good a place as any to spend the night. When he'd picked out a house at the edge of the village for billets, the half-tracks took tactical positions one to either side of it where they could also see each other, and he told the middle-aged woman who came to the door of the house to watch them that she and her family would have to leave the house and move in with neighbors for a while.

This wasn't the first time he'd appropriated a house, but doing it still didn't feel good. However, when the woman said she had a son upstairs who was unwell, he told her in his school German that had grown quite competent in recent months that he was sorry, but that they didn't expect to be here long. He'd told her she had fifteen minutes to assemble whatever she needed for the night, and in less time than that, two boys perhaps eight and ten bolted out of the house and fled down the road. The woman and another younger woman came out then more slowly, supporting the ailing son between them with his arms across their shoulders. He was wearing a striped collarless shirt, and from the waist down he was wrapped in a blanket pinned closed like a skirt. His bare ankles and his feet in carpet slippers were visible below the blanket. The three of them walked with their eyes on the ground, as if picking their way but also Ben had thought in a kind of scorn. When they came abreast of where he was waiting in his jeep, the older woman looked up long enough to say, "You will surely be gone in the morning?"

"I think so," he said.

He remained in the jeep for a while still, watching the trio move slowly down the road with the man all but dragged by the two women. The slow shuffle of his feet suggested loco- motion but really wasn't. When they stopped once, he leaned against a tree and disengaged his arms from the women's shoul- ders to allow them to rest, and Sergeant Riley, sitting in the driver's seat of the jeep next to Ben, said, "That was a thirty caliber germ bit that mother-fucker."

"I suppose," Ben said.

"Piss-poor shooting too," Riley said.

Riley's voice, which had always been distinctively gentle, had had a harsh edge a lot of the time in the past few months since he'd been witness to the death of his younger brother in the Hürtgen Forest. He'd heard that the brother's unit was on the line somewhere near Schmidt, and he'd taken a jeep one day, gone to look for him, and found the unit just as the medics were bringing his body into the clearing station. He'd run over a shoe mine in a personnel carrier, and though he was entirely recognizable still, Riley said, he was jumbled up inside like a busted clock. Riley had been AWOL for three days then, drunk in a whorehouse in Verviers most of the time, and when the mp's picked him up he was talking his head off to a fagged blonde who'd probably come to consider this kind of listening just another of her regular services. He must have talked him- self out to her however, for he'd made little direct reference to his brother's death since he'd been back aside from telling Ben what had happened. Consciousness of it was obviously still boiling around in his head though.

"Let's go see if we can't liberate something to eat that's better than K-rations," Ben said to change the subject. "I've got Spam coming out of my ears."

"Suits me, Lieutenant," Riley said.

Inside the house, in the kitchen, they found eggs and sau- sages, home-baked bread, and jars of pickles. They weren't supposed to take food belonging to civilians, but they did regularly, and one of the men from the half-track crews had also turned up an extensive wine-cellar. It was getting to be an old war, and when he went upstairs after eating to select a bed for himself and investigate the possibility of a bath—a luxury he hadn't enjoyed for weeks—he wasn't surprised to find a major's uniform hanging in a wardrobe in the largest of the bedrooms. The well-supplied kitchen and the wine implied a certain level of privilege.

He'd even learned by then how to deal with the kind of wood-fired water-heater he found in the bathroom. But when he'd stripped and shaved and was waiting for the tub to fill, some understanding of his situation pierced this superficial security, maybe because the splash of the water into the tub cut him off from the sounds of conversation downstairs, and he suddenly felt acutely what he was—a man alone in his skin in bad circumstances.

He pulled aside the blackout blind over the window and in the moonlight he could see his jeep and the two radio vehicles drawn up under cover of the trees next to the house, and beyond them, in a field, one of the half-tracks under a camouflage net. Three girls had materialized next to the house too, and Brennan, one of the radio operators, was leading one of them off into the shrubbery. Brennan had a reputation to sustain. On Omaha Beach on the afternoon of D-Day, he was reputed to have asked his platoon sergeant where he could find a pro station.

Calm, moonlit, this was a military version of pastoral. All was in a fashion well. But soon after he got into the tub, he heard someone yell "Halt," then feet moving under the window and the door of the house opening and closing. A moment later, Riley called up the staircase, "We've got a baby Kraut down here, Lieutenant."

"A soldier?" he asked.

"You might say."

"Okay, hold on to him. I'll be down soon."

"No problem holding on to him," Riley shouted. "We couldn't get rid of him without shooting him first. Take your time."

He dried himself on a tablecloth because he hadn't been able to locate any towels, and when he got downstairs, he found a very young German soldier, a boy really, backed into a corner of the kitchen with half a dozen men in an amused semi-circle around him. Riley pinched the boy's arm and said, "A nice tender one, Lieutenant. Just about right to roast with an apple in his mouth. A little skinny maybe, but not stringy."

The men laughed uncomfortably, but there was something porcine about the boy even though he also looked emaciated. His skin was white and pink, his face was round with small marble eyes, a nose flat at the bridge and flared at the nostrils, and a small pouting mouth. When Ben appeared, his body stiffened, and after a brief hesitation he snapped a vibrant salute. The other men moved apart, but Riley didn't relinquish his place near the boy who kept flinching from him as though he expected something worse to follow that demonstrative pinch. "Does he understand English?" Ben asked.

"Not so you'd notice," Riley said, and the boy said, *"Nein, nein, kein Englisch,"* with a desperation that suggested that this was only one of many things he could have used and didn't possess.

"I guess his English is up to my German," someone said.

The boy was listening intently, but it was impossible to know what he did understand. When Ben asked him his name in German however, he answered promptly and with evident relief, "Walther Muhler."

"Rank?" Ben continued.

"Private."

"Number?"

He gave that too, the answers coming almost before the prescribed questions were completed. Probably he wanted to show how entirely ready he was to cooperate, though a childish eagerness to excel might also have helped account for this speed. He couldn't have been quite as young as he'd looked at first glance, but the hair on his face was too soft still to make a razor rasp. When he was asked what unit he belonged to, a question, unlike the previous ones, that the Geneva convention didn't require him to answer, he promptly gave the number of a home guard division anyway, and Ben asked, "Where is your division now?"

"I don't know."

"What do you mean you don't know?"

"I don't know," he repeated. He probably was and had been telling the truth, and expecting the truth to please, didn't understand why he should now have caused displeasure.

"Well, where have you come from?" Ben asked.

He didn't know that either, he said, but feeling possibly that he was believed again, he went on spontaneously to unfold his recent history, telling it with a child's adherence to detail, almost without selection or emphasis. About a week ago, he said, his company had been assigned to a defense line in a forest. They'd come there in trucks at night and he didn't know the name of the forest but a section of autobahn ran through it. They'd built some roadblocks, and placed demolition charges under a bridge but hadn't blown it. Then four days ago they'd been told they were to move, to Kassel, where the division was reassembling for a new offensive.

"But the Americans already had Kassel four days ago," Ben said. "I was in Kassel more than four days ago."

"Yes?" the boy said. His eyes were bulging with confusion.

"Okay, go on," Ben said.

He continued, but his account was slowed now by a recurrent falter of uncertainty. His squad had been left behind in the forest as a special detail, he said. Each man was given a bazooka, and they were stationed singly on the high bank over the autobahn with instructions to let concentrations of enemy vehicles go by, but fire on single vehicles or small groups of vehicles. They were to hold these positions until night, when they would be relieved.

He lay on the bank all day, cradling the long pipe of the bazooka in his arms. Once a column of American tanks crashed by at great speed, and he flattened down in the underbrush and prayed. The tank hatches were open, and even over the infernal noise of the tracks and the engines, he'd heard the radios, and the voices of men talking and laughing. The tanks were followed by some trucks that were less noisy, and a black man in one of the trucks was singing *"Deutschland, Deutschland, über alles."* That had confused him. He'd never seen a black man before.

The rest of the day though, he'd seen no human life at all. Once he rolled over onto a bees' nest and was stung. Another time he saw a rabbit only a few meters from him cropping grass and thought of shooting it, but didn't for fear the noise would bring more Americans or alarm his comrades. When he was hungry, he ate some of his rations cold, afraid to build a fire to warm them.

He waited anxiously for his relief as it grew dark, but he soon began to suspect—he related this with an awed hush of mystery—that something had gone wrong. Finally, around two in the morning when his relief had still not arrived, he set out to contact the man to his left. He walked more than a kilometer and found no one, though he did find a pile of bazooka shells where he assumed a man had been posted. When he back-tracked then and tried to find the man to his right, he again found no one. He realized therefore that he'd been abandoned, and in anger at the treachery of his comrades, and in great fear, he decided to desert and find some way to give himself up to the Americans. He was pretty sure he said that it would be safer to give himself up than wait to be captured.

He'd set out cautiously, walking only at night and vigilantly even then to avoid chance patrols either American or German by either of whom he knew he might be shot. He hoped to come on some American headquarters where he thought he could count on fair treatment rather than on just a few soldiers who might be less dependable. But a headquarters hadn't been easy to find, he said, and he became more and more terrified the longer he had to search. He'd lived on the remnants of his rations and whatever he could find to eat in the woods which wasn't much. Too frightened and hungry to sleep much either, he simply lay down under whatever cover was at hand each dawn, and stayed there until darkness released him to travel again. He'd spent the previous day only a couple of kilometers from this village, and had come on here after dark meaning, though he hadn't done this before, to knock at some door and ask for food. He'd finished his rations, and he had to do something about that, he couldn't go on any longer on an empty stomach. Hunger had made him stupid though he said. It hadn't even occurred to him that there might already be Americans here. It was just luck that he'd seen one of the half-tracks in the moonlight before the soldiers in it had seen him. He'd quickly pulled out the piece of white cloth that he'd found somewhere in his wanderings and saved for such an occasion, and attached it to a stick. He hadn't intended to give himself up in such a careless fashion, but in the end he'd been thinking with his stomach and not with his head.

Like a pig, Ben thought, relieved to find some characterological basis for the appearance of that pale, globular, dirt-streaked but essentially pink and white face with its small round eyes, round mouth, and snub nose. The boy really was repellent, and whatever compassion he felt for him as he heard his story was pretty minimal. But he must also, he thought now in retrospect, have been more fascinated by his fear than he quite knew. Why otherwise would he have asked, "Did you really come all this way alone, without anyone to help you?"

"Yes, all alone," the boy said, and it was as if this made him realize something he hadn't quite absorbed before. "All alone, all alone," he repeated, and began to sob, his cheeks laved suddenly not just with tears but with the sweat of fear as well. He was exuding water like a squeezed sponge.

"What's he blubbering about?" Riley asked.

"He says he's been all alone for days," Ben said, embarrassed as he said it.

"Shit!" Riley said.

One of the men muttered that he had something to do, and there was a general exodus through the blackout curtain and the door behind it. Ben and Riley were left alone with their prisoner who was wiping his nose on his already filthy green wool sleeve and trying to suppress wet sobs. "What do you aim to do with him?" Riley asked.

"Turn him over to the mp's first chance we get," Ben said.

"We haven't seen an mp for two days now," Riley said, "and it may be another week before we see one again the way we're going."

"I suppose that's right."

"Well then?"

"I guess we'll just have to tote him around with us until we do see some mp's."

"Jesus, Lieutenant!"

Riley was turgid with anger, and the boy eyed them anxiously over the sleeve pressed to his snotty nose. Standing in a slouch that caused his stomach to protrude, he followed their conversation back and forth assiduously. Even if he could understand English no better than Riley did German, he must have suspected what they were talking about, and his eyes, made even smaller by his crying, were hard points of brightness in the watery waste of his face.

"We can't cart him around with us, Lieutenant," Riley said. "We've got too much else to worry about already."

"What's the alternative?" Ben asked.

"Turn him loose again. Why not? You could call that an act of charity. I'll walk him up to the woods and tell him to beat it."

He'd been ready to accept that at first as a welcome solution. A prisoner was a nuisance they didn't need right then, and this particular prisoner was making his flesh crawl. The boy made him uneasy in some way he didn't quite understand, but absolutely didn't need. "Okay," he said, "take him before it gets any later."

"Sure thing, Lieutenant," Riley said, and then to the boy he said, "Outside!"

That he said it in German might have made it sound particularly threatening. *"Heraus!"* It could have been the only word of German Riley knew. Anyway, the boy seemed to take it as a considered, mortal sentence. *"Nein, bitte nein!"* he said, directing his appeal to Ben.

Riley wasn't any longer having Ben as an intermediary however. His voice was louder, harsher, and less controlled when he repeated his order, and he swallowed the first syllable. *" 'raus!"* He'd also drawn the Luger he'd acquired recently out of its shoulder holster and was waving the boy toward the blackout- curtained door with it. And for the moment anyway, Muhler gave up. He trotted across the kitchen and behind the curtain with his face once more exuding water.

Ben could feel not only the intensity of his relief when he could no longer see them, but also its fragility. He didn't really believe the boy would turn loose. When Riley released him on the hillside at the edge of the woods, he'd just circle and come back, perhaps in the morning before they headed out again in pursuit of two radio signals the sources of which would be moving apart. But a lot sooner than this could happen, he heard what he knew was the drop of the safety on a pistol, and when he was outside the door—after tangling interminably first in the curtain—he saw Riley in preternaturally sharp outline in bright white moonlight, pointing the Luger at the boy who was lying in bright green grass at his feet. Riley was screaming at him to get up before he blew his ass off.

So weak-kneed he could barely stand himself, awash in what he thought was fear that he was already too late but that must have been all the fear that had been accumulating unrecognized for days, he called Riley's name. He could hear that his voice was faint, but when he called a second time, Riley slowly thumbed the safety closed and returned the pistol decisively to its black leather holster under his left armpit. "Okay, Lieutenant," he said, "the lily-livered son-of-a-bitch is all yours. Just don't ask me to deal with him again though. Not in any way."

Ben had said that was fair enough, which it was. But he was too unsettled to sleep when he went to bed. He kept thinking he was about to throw up the fresh eggs and homemade sausages he'd had for supper, and thinking then about the mess that would make in the deep dusty featherbed he'd appropriated in the principal bedroom in which he could detect the olfactory records of generations, odors that weren't so much strong as complex. Meanwhile the boy was sleeping like a baby on the floor next to the bed, making up for all the sleep he'd recently missed. It was obvious that no precautions had to be taken with him. He wasn't about to go anywhere, or to do anything but sleep. And when he accompanied them the next morning in the back seat of Ben's jeep, his relief at having effected his own rescue was as abject as his terror had been the previous evening. Prolonged exposure to such unmodulated feeling—the boy's relief as threatening as his fear—would have been hard to tolerate, but by luck in the middle of the morning they encountered some mp's from the armored division escorting a column of prisoners rearward. When the mp's allowed Muhler to be turned over to them, Ben could lapse back to a level of misery to which he was more accustomed.

12

FAITH'S PULSE when he'd taken it last a couple of hours ago—
it must have been about two-thirty, just after Sarah left—had
still been discouragingly faint. But it had been neither dramatically fast nor dramatically slow and it had been fairly
regular, undisrupted by the fibrillations that had felt to him
at other times like suppressed cries of mortal distress. It was
a little more than forty-eight hours since he'd felt them first,
shortly after his return from Massingham when he'd taken
his initial shift on this round-the-clock vigil that he, Lucky,
and Sarah were conducting. That first time had been the
most disturbing. Since then either they'd been less extreme or
he was simply readier to have that faint seismographic line
broken suddenly while he was intent on counting and timing
by an irregular succession of violent beats that made his count
meaningless. Hard flutters, sometimes bangs, they followed
no pattern his ignorant fingers could establish, and they seemed
to explode into his own body without intercession from the
thin tissues of Faith's frail wrist. But even without taking her
pulse, he could tell that her heart was no longer doing its
essential work very well. She was still present by only the
thinnest margin, and her face, above the two pillows on which
her head was elevated to facilitate breathing, was so minimized,
its irreducible structure so little mitigated or disguised, the

chalky skin all but transparent, that just looking at her felt like an intrusive act.

Some obscure change had now taken place though in her appearance or his response to it or both after two days in the course of which he'd been at her bedside more often than not, much of the time looking for any sign of change on that finely reduced face which struck him as beautiful still whenever he could for any time separate its appearance from the commanding polarities of sickness and health, life and death. And since she scarcely moved at all, he was much more aware of her face than he was of her vestigial body. Her apartment was kept very warm, but even under the thin blanket and sheet that was therefore sufficient—and anything more would have seemed crushingly heavy—her body was visible only in minimal relief. Her face, by contrast, was in high relief, the skin stretched back tight from her nose to her cheekbones and from her chin to her throat.

It had been an arduous couple of days, but what was odd about what he'd been doing was first how un-odd it had come to seem, how expectable, and second how fully employed it allowed him to feel. Both more fully and less arbitrarily than by anything else he'd done in a long time. He'd thought about this particularly after Charlie Coleman had called the previous day to find out what had happened at Massingham and to say that he'd concluded after further thought that nothing done about this business now might matter very much if it was already "in the realm of the discretionary." It might that is all depend finally on what their friend in the Department wanted to make of whatever he did or didn't know.

"The realm of the discretionary" sounded like a poor place to be, particularly if the discretion that ruled the realm was Marvin's. And what Lucky, Sarah, and he were doing right now was in some exactly different, some non-discretionary

realm. He didn't have to think too much yet about the implications of this. It was enough right now to know it, and to
know also that their all but unquestioning confidence that,
together, they were doing something reasonable and inevitable
that they were able, ready, and wished to do, was attributable
in large part to Lucky's clarity in advance about how this
anticipatable occasion was to be met when it came. She'd talked
it out carefully at different times with Faith, and she'd also
talked to Phil about how to be as sure as they could be that
Faith was suffering no more pain than was unavoidable. Lucky
had phoned Phil again a couple of times in the past couple of
days for further advice, but she'd also told him—as she'd told
Ben and Sarah, and Mark too when she called him—that she
didn't believe this was the ultimate crisis. She was sure enough
that it wasn't to think Phil and Mark needn't come east now.
Her mother had really wanted them all to get together for her
birthday—wanted it sufficiently, she thought, for that to bring
her back now for a few more weeks anyway—and since they
both had busy lives and couldn't commute to Boston, they'd
do better to wait until then. Meanwhile, she was confident
that she, Ben, and Sarah could do all there was to be done
without assistance.

The crisis had developed with alarming speed however. Lucky
had reported only worrisome signs when Ben had spoken to
her from the diner in Massingham, and he hadn't even at first
registered anything significantly different about the quality of
her worry this time from what it had been any number of
times in the past year or more when she'd thought her mother
was worse or weaker. Initially, even her irritability only suggested that she no longer attached much importance to his trip
to Massingham. That hadn't done much in turn for his own
uncertain hope that seeing Peter Drew would be useful, and
the actual interview then certainly hadn't been a great success.
Drew himself though—his invented persona that belonged to

some non-existent border country, his situation, the quality
of his attachment to the Miller Labs postcard, the classy prop-
osition with which he'd concluded their talk—had been in-
trinsically interesting, and it had been interesting too then to
remember suddenly in the middle of his drive home why the
name Massingham had begun to ring a tantalizingly familiar
bell for him soon after he'd seen it on the label at Jake's the
previous afternoon. It was only after these interests had begun
to fade and he had nothing immediate to occupy him but the
nearly automatic activity of driving, that the quality of the
disturbance in Lucky's voice began to come back to him as
somehow distinctive. The apprehension this generated built
up rapidly however, so that he wasn't really startled to find
Sarah with Lucky when he got home.

Lucky had come through the connecting door from Faith's
apartment when she heard him arrive, and told him what there
was to know. Annie had called her at the office that afternoon
to say that Faith had complained of being tired and had gone
back to bed right after her lunch. She was just going to rest
on top of the bed, she said, and didn't want to be undressed
again. But she also called a friend who was to visit her that
afternoon and asked her to come another time. Faith was awake
on the bed reading when she left, Annie said, but she suspected
she'd gone to sleep as soon as she was alone. Her pulse had
been a little weaker again too and she'd been fibrillating some.
Nothing dramatic, but in conjunction with her fatigue this was
a little alarming. Lucky had gone home soon after Annie's call
and found Faith as predicted asleep on the bed. It had been
hard to wake her enough to get her clothes off and get her into
a nightgown and back into bed. And since then, except for a
few brief intervals, she'd been asleep.

Lucky's plan, fully formed by the time Ben returned, was
to call in no medical assistance—no doctors or nurses except
for Annie who would continue to come in for her usual couple

of hours each day. Either she or Ben or Sarah however, and whenever possible two of them together, were to stay with Faith at all times, not only to watch her but to be both audible and visible to her whenever she was sufficiently conscious for that to be possible. Which might of course, Lucky said, be more often than they knew. They were to go shifts as they could. She could certainly stay away from her office for a few days, or just duck in briefly if there was anything that couldn't wait, and Sarah too was going to arrange the next few days so that she'd spend only a few hours each day in her office, and would work in Faith's room instead on a brief she had to prepare.

It was obviously only a short range plan which they'd have to rethink if the crisis was protracted. But Lucky didn't think it would be protracted, even as, she repeated, she didn't think it was the ultimate event. She was sure Faith would wish it not to be, and that that had to matter. Her thought therefore was that they could encourage that wish by keeping as much going on around Faith as possible, working as Sarah would be in her room, talking to each other as freely as they could manage to, talking to Faith herself whenever she was even somewhat awake, having their meals together near her.

Certain minimal tasks too were to be performed as regularly as possible. They were to help Faith take some nourishment whenever she was able and at all inclined to, and to try particularly to see that she took her prescribed medications. But mostly she insisted they were just to be there, to remind her mother that she really did wish to stay alive a while longer.

Before when Ben had heard Lucky talk about or allude to her belief in the determining importance of her mother's birthday, this had generally seemed wishful or notional to him, and could make him impatient. But in the course of the past two days, as he'd fallen in with her plan, some of the time at least it had seemed persuasive, maybe because the stress of the occasion failed either to weaken Lucky's judgment or to make it strident. But he did wonder at times too whether fatigue hadn't put him in a mesmerized state of acceptance. He'd gone to bed for a few hours just after he got home from Massingham, and he'd slept again for a couple of hours each night since then, before midnight. But otherwise, he'd been in Faith's apartment continuously. He was spending somewhat more time here than either Lucky or Sarah, since there was nothing else he had to do, and it had been his idea to take the midnight to six a.m. shift tonight alone and give them both a chance for some sleep. He'd been alone with Faith now consequently for almost five hours, except for the half hour or so when Sarah had come in unexpectedly to join him. He remembered from standing guard duty in the army that the hardest time to fight off sleep was always around three or four o'clock in the morning, and that difficulty was exacerbated now when his only responsibility was to pay close attention to someone who was asleep.

He'd been alert enough though still around two when Sarah had come across from the other apartment where he'd supposed her to be asleep to see how Faith was doing. Earlier, she said, when she'd been in here with Lucky, she'd had some impression that her condition was changing. She couldn't really have said why she thought this, but there was so little to watch now when you watched Faith, her vital signs were so faint and few, that after a while you might well become aware of something too slight to name. "I found myself awake anyway," she said, "and thought I'd ask whether you had any similar impression—and, incidentally, see how you were doing over here alone."

"I can't say I've been aware of any difference," he said, "except that she hasn't been fibrillating when I've taken her pulse."

"Well, that's something. She wasn't at her worst when Mom

and I were with her, but she was definitely still knocking at times."

She'd settled down on the other chair by the bed then as though she meant to stay a while, and he said, "You're not going to use your chance to get some sleep while you can?"

"After a bit maybe," she said. "When I woke up a few minutes ago, I was wide awake, and the idea of company was very appealing. It still is. I don't seem to be a natural breeder, do I? Twenty minutes pregnant, and I'm having trouble both eating and sleeping."

"Isn't the eating part pretty much par for the course," he said cautiously, "and doesn't it generally only last a few weeks? But if I remember correctly, your trouble sleeping is counter-indicated. Is that the right term? I mean, anyway, that I'd be inclined to think something else was causing it."

The familiar mocking smile that concentrated in one corner of her mouth had appeared as soon as he began to talk, but she actually laughed as he finished, he assumed at his caution. "You're a good thinker," she said. "It could be plain anxiety that's at fault, or it could be a mix of anxiety and anticipation."

"Oh?" he said, inviting her to go on. He'd been aware already that she was eating very little, and several times he'd heard her say something about her stomach being finicky. And he figured this was all but inevitable. She'd always been the one of their children most likely to get carsick or seasick, or to stop eating when she was worried. Her skin had always lost its customary dark healthy look too when she was afflicted this way and taken on the greenish cast that gave an almost phosphorescent glow to her face now in artificial light. But he'd been uneasily aware as well watching her of a kind of physical discouragement that was less ordinary. Every move she made seemed effortful.

It could only exacerbate the uneasiness this caused him to

remember that Lucky had always prospered right from the start when she was pregnant, and for the first few months too she was likely to sleep more than she was awake. About halfway through then this changed, and her energy came booming back. That consistent, positive response to pregnancy had contributed a lot in fact to the difficulty they'd had deciding ultimately to have no more children. The decision had been made under pressure. Sarah was just past two when Lucky got pregnant again. It was unintentional, but it wasn't entirely unwanted, and they'd had to review painfully and repeatedly all the considerations that made it a bad idea. Having three fine healthy children already, wasn't it pushing their luck to count on having a fourth? And what about the logistical and financial complications? They already needed a larger house, and they'd just begun to look at private schools for Phil. And so on.

The limitation to all these considerations however, as Lucky pointed out, was that they were only cautionary and hypothetical. What was certain was that they both loved having kids, and that she also loved being pregnant. She felt better pregnant than she ever did otherwise. Not just better about herself either. It was much more immediate and physical. She felt fantastically well. Ben was too unsure of what he really wanted to try to persuade her of anything, but what had tipped the scale finally nonetheless was his saying that he wasn't sure he had sufficient imaginative space left for another child.

"I wish I believed it was just thinking about Faith that was making it hard for me to sleep," Sarah said after a moment, "but I know that's not true. Actually, what's happening to her, or how it's happening at least, seems pretty wonderful to me, no matter which way it's going this time. If this isn't, as Mom says, the 'ultimate occasion,' that occasion when it comes isn't going to be much different. I'm really going to miss her when she is gone, but right now part of me envies her. I can't imagine having a life that would end this way, so completed. But it also began to occur to me when I woke up a little while ago, that not everyone would respond to this the way we're responding. Or, particularly, the way we're responding to it together. I started thinking about Carl, who should turn up here before long, and I could imagine him thinking the kind of melancholy exhilaration in which he's going to find us joined a little odd. Carl's not essentially an accepter."

"We don't have much alternative to acceptance right now," Ben said.

"Of course," Sarah said. "That's true. And Carl probably wouldn't be any readier than Mom is to call in the health establishment. But the difference is that we flourish on acceptance and he doesn't. Absence of an alternative doesn't necessarily lead him to reconciliation. He's a lot less likely than we are to find dignity in things as they are, and he's become remarkably accustomed by now to trying to go two ways at once. That's a lot of the reason he's so nerved up so much of the time."

Discomforted by the intensity with which Sarah was talking, Ben had shifted his eyes to Faith for a moment, and had a sudden intimation when he did that Sarah had been correct. That Faith wasn't quite as she had been. Like Sarah too, he couldn't have said why this was so, but her state seemed more like true sleep now, seemed to be recuperative rather than part of a process of failure.

"I woke up scared first," Sarah said, "and that certainly wasn't for Faith. It must have been for myself. Because I knew Carl's arrival was imminent."

"I wasn't expecting him back quite that soon," Ben said, but was aware as he said it that he'd scarcely thought about Carl at all since he'd gotten back from Massingham. Even that Carl would be the father of Sarah's child had had little place in his consciousness in the past couple of days. It was as though once she'd moved in with him and Lucky, her pregnancy, like Faith's dying, was a matter of concern only to the members of the household.

"He wasn't supposed to be," Sarah said, "but his Guatemala venture has turned out not to be much to his liking. He says the politics of it stink, and that the work is being even more corruptly administered than he'd assumed it would be. So he's cut out, and though under the circumstances—my circumstances I mean as well as Faith's—it will be nice to have him back sooner than he was supposed to be, the mood in which he's likely to arrive may not be so nice. Money's one of the many ticklish issues between us. It's not something he thinks about a lot, but he doesn't like the idea of my making more than he does, of his not paying his own share, and since he's now breaking his contract, he'll be paid only for the time he's spent working down there, and won't be reimbursed for his travel expenses. That's why he's not coming back on a regular scheduled flight. He shopped around, and managed to get booked on a charter flight from Guatemala City to New York that's bottom price. But it's apparently bottom priority too which may be why he was able to get onto it. The schedule was still unclear when I talked to him last, but he hoped he might be getting into Newark sometime about now. That very likely has something to do with why I woke up. I've left a message for him at Newark which he may or may not of course get, to come here when he arrives in Boston. At best, that won't be for some hours. Only don't be surprised if the bell rings at an unlikely time."

There'd been a charged intermission then when he was all but certain that Sarah had something more still she might say but that it was touch and go whether she would and that nothing he could say was likely to better the chances. She was wrapped in a quilted robe she'd borrowed from Lucky. Considerably too large for her, it padded out her body, made it diffuse, but also made her face look disproportionately small by contrast, and concentrated. "Being scared," she said finally, "isn't an emotion that's absolutely unknown to me, but as I get older I'm scared less and less often—and I also like it when it does happen less and less. I have good reason to be scared this time however. It was no accident that I got pregnant, but it was unexpected nonetheless. I hadn't been doing anything not to get pregnant for over a year. Carl knew that, but he'd also let me know that that was my decision, not ours. He's not at all sure he's ready to have a baby—or, therefore, that we are. But he also wasn't going to tell me what he thought I should do about that. We had what might be called an unsatisfactory understanding which could be seen as one more instance of Carl's wearing capacity to more or less go two ways at once. When nothing happened anyway, we stopped talking about it, only that of course didn't lead to any further understanding. And now suddenly I am pregnant, and all I know for sure is that I'm not going to terminate the pregnancy."

This was more than Ben had learned previously from Lucky. More probably than Lucky had known, and there were good reasons why Sarah might talk to him about Carl more than she did to Lucky—reasons that were increasingly palpable as they continued to talk. They weren't really having a conversation though. Mostly Sarah was telling him what it was like to be caught between two needs neither of which she was willingly going to deny. She wanted a baby no matter how Carl reacted when he found out she was pregnant, and she wanted Carl too no matter how pissed-off she was at him. She had no way of knowing therefore what was going to happen, and that was scary. She probably wouldn't have gotten preg-

nant if she hadn't believed that sometimes the idea of having
a kid meant as much to Carl as it did to her. But he might
very well nonetheless say he still wasn't ready to be a father
and couldn't be certain that he ever would be. She knew he
wasn't sure to begin with that he was or ever would be ready
to lead what might be called an ordinary life—which was of
course what all the *Sturm und Drang* about the damn fellowship
was about. The idea both did and didn't appeal to him—
sometimes alternately and sometimes simultaneously. Money
really did mean less to him than it did to most people she
knew, but since he also didn't like to be beholden, the idea of
steady work would have to be painfully in the air now when
having quit the job in Guatemala might mean that he'd have
less money in his bank account when he returned than he'd
had when he left. And yet if that revived his interest in the
fellowship, it wouldn't be a healthy revival. She was the one
who wanted him to lead a more regular life. She didn't care
whether he made less money than she did. She was in an
overpaid profession, and she'd be happy to be the major wage-
earner in the family indefinitely. But she did want him to be
around most of the time, and she wasn't the least bit sure that
that was the kind of life he wanted. Or again, she was afraid
he generally didn't but sometimes did. He didn't really possess
the constitution, psychic or physical, for the kind of life he
had a yen for, which was of course one reason that kind of a
life was so attractive to him. He had little affection for doing
what came easy. One way and another, she said, he was a
very volatile mix of incompatibles that she found both compelling and sometimes impossible.

After the freighted pause when Ben hadn't known whether
she was going to say anything more, this had come in a torrent.
Now though she checked herself and shifted mode. The question this time seemed to be not whether to say what she knew,

but rather how to say what she was less clear about. "I guess you can see," she said, "that if this description makes Carl sound a little crazy, I must be at least as crazy as he is. It takes two to tango, and we've been doing some very complicated steps together. What woke me up a little while ago wasn't just being scared. It was also being nerved-up suddenly in a lot of different ways for which the strange calm of the past couple of days had done a lot to unprepare me. All those built-in contradictions in Carl's character are obvious, and I'm pretty sure they're what attracted me to him right from the beginning. You remember, Dad, when you brought him in from the street that night after the fracas that took place right in front of our door."

"When he had a persistent nose-bleed, but kept on talking all the time Lucky was putting cold compresses across his face to stop it."

"Exactly," Sarah said. "Until then, my idea of heroes came mostly from the *Iliad* and the *Odyssey*, and I never liked Homer's heroes very much. But now it occurred to me that a hero could also be pretty frail and that was a lot more appealing. Being a hero if you already had the attributes of a hero, like Achilles or Hercules, hadn't seemed as remarkable to me as doing what you weren't really equipped to do.

"There's something crazy about that way of thinking of course. You and Mom always encouraged us to find something we could do and do it, and that makes a lot of sense. It's what each of the three of us has eventually gotten around to also, some of us faster and some more slowly. We ought to be grateful to you for that, and I think we are. But Carl brought out some other sense of possibility for me that I can't quite relinquish either."

Sarah had managed to say all that she had to say in less than half an hour. The isolation had probably made that possible, Ben thought, and the absolute absence of any distraction with

Faith deep in her semblance of sleep. The impression Carl had
made on her that first evening had stayed with her, she'd told
him, all through that time starting a few years later when the
consistent trouble she was having in a succession of different
involvements and relationships none of which lasted very long
was that she never felt very involved in any of them. She'd
already begun to believe that dissatisfaction in a variety of
forms was to be her portion when she and Carl met again, on
their own, when he and Ben were no longer in much touch
with each other. She'd known then pretty quickly that what
she had with Carl was what she'd been missing before even
though things were never easy between them. What was particularly not easy—was in fact very hard, she'd said, and she
was sure Ben had to be aware of this too—was that Carl could
seem so very much like one of them, almost a member of their
family, and yet the better you got to know him the more you
discovered how much he wasn't like them at all. She and Carl
could more or less agree intellectually about almost anything
of importance they talked about, but nervously and dynami-
cally, operatively, they as often as not ended up miles apart.
That was trying, but it was also inescapably compelling. "It's
like a legal and even maybe a salutary form of incest," Sarah
had said. "What could be more desirable—if, that is, it turned
out to be negotiable. I grew up with an image of life much
quieter on average than any life I'm ever likely to have with
Carl. That difference isn't going to be easy to accept, but at
the same time, I know, it's what I'm drawn to. So in my own
way I have to be judged at least as crazy as Carl."

Sarah had gone back then to try again to get some sleep,
not to be wiped-out in advance she said before Carl had even
arrived, and once she was gone, quiet, which had assumed
summary figurative importance when she'd talked about the
kind of life she'd been brought up to expect, became an acute,
immediate, literal matter for Ben. Accumulated fatigue was

rapidly diminishing his capacity for attention just when attention might be most necessary if, as Sarah had first suggested and he'd then thought quite possible, Faith's condition was changing. She'd awakened once in the early evening, Lucky and Sarah had reported, though they all knew it was probably an exaggeration to call these episodes awakenings. Faith was hardly conscious when they occurred. But she'd apparently opened her eyes and responded sufficiently to what was said to her, or just to the suggestions of touch, to take her medications and a few sips of milk before drifting off again. All the time he'd been with her though her sleep had been unbroken except by occasional minor perturbations, but he didn't want to miss even minor changes in this extended state which wasn't actually true sleep any more than her awakenings were true awakenings. Each belonged to some more problematic condition. Nothing was changing obviously enough now though to counteract his fatigue, and the idea of reading aloud to her occurred to him first chiefly as an alternative to the otherwise near-absolute quiet.

Among the relatively few books Faith hadn't given away or sold when she disposed of most of her belongings before moving into this apartment was a collected Dickens in twenty-odd volumes that had belonged to her husband. It was a good early-twentieth-century edition in faded green bindings, and Ben walked over to the bookcase where the line of uniform spines stood out conspicuously among the disparate single volumes and let his eye run along the titles, past the two volumes of the Forster *Life* and the two volumes of *Sketches by Boz* to the first volume of *Pickwick*. The very feel of the book when he drew it from the shelf was encouraging, the worn patina of the cloth and the way the flat spine lay in the cup of his palm. When he sat down again and opened it, the heavy paper leaves, still securely stitched, opened as though on oiled hinges, and the type was large and black. And the citation in the first paragraph of the Transactions of the Pickwick Club as evidence of the ensuing story's truth was reassuring too.

He began to read aloud then at the beginning of Chapter 2 when Mr. Samuel Pickwick arises at first light on the morning of the thirteenth of May one thousand eight hundred and twenty-seven and looking to right and left on Goswell Street "as far as the eye could reach," decides that he really can no longer "be content to gaze on Goswell Street forever, without one effort to penetrate to the hidden countries which on every side surround it." This was a Sakhalin Island to his own scale or range of possibility, Ben thought, the adventure of a quiet life, and though he hadn't looked at *Pickwick* for years, he found what he was reading familiar almost word by word. The ire of the cab driver who assumes when he sees that Pickwick has been entering the various irreverent things he's been saying in a notebook that his passenger is preparing a report for the police. Then the appearance as peace-maker of Alfred Jingle in a bottle-green coat altogether too small for him but particularly short in the sleeves. Ben remembered without exception the anecdotes appropriate to each passing occasion that Jingle begins to recount in his economical tele-graphese as soon as he and the Pickwickians have taken their places together on the stagecoach. It was all so vivid that it did seem secretly possible to him for a time that the wasted, remote figure on the bed, equally affected, might really be summoned back by recollection as he read: " 'Heads, heads— take care of your heads!' cried the loquacious stranger as they came out under the low archway, which in those days formed the entrance to the coach-yard. 'Terrible place—dangerous work—other day—five children—mother—tall lady eating sandwiches—forgot the arch—crash—knock—children look round—mother's head off—sandwich in her hand—no mouth to put it in—head of a family off—shocking, shocking!' "

He'd been reading in a restrained voice, not to sound too

much an idiot even to himself in the otherwise utter still-
ness, but he might not have been able to maintain his restraint
at this point if he hadn't looked across at Faith's lucid face
expectantly and seen no reaction whatsoever. Her face was
animated only by the barely perceptible, slow alternation of
inhalation and exhalation. Chastened, dropped from an absurd
high, he continued to read only another few lines aloud, through
Pickwick's too aptly concluding response to Jingle's story: " 'I
am ruminating,' said Mr. Pickwick, 'on the strange mutability
of human affairs.' "

He continued to read to himself a while longer then, but
found it less and less possible to remain attentive, not to drift
away from the page, and he finally stopped trying somewhere in the middle of the account of how Jingle, dressed in
Mr. Winkle's surreptitiously borrowed Pickwick Club jacket,
insults Dr. Slammer at the ball. At about this point the disposition to drift suddenly became very particular.

The last time he'd read these pages aloud must he realized
have been, in both like and grotesquely different circumstances, the night Mark was born. Mark's early life had been a lot
more troubled than either Phil's or Sarah's, and this had been
true even of his entry into the world. Lucky was in labor with
him at least twice as long as she'd been with Phil, so that the
difficulty was exacerbated by contrast. Her labor had started
early one morning, and by the middle of that evening she was
pretty battered. He'd decided to read to her then, to give her
something else to think about between contractions, and in the
lounge at the end of the hospital corridor, among the old *New
Yorker*s and *Atlantic*s piled on a table, he'd discovered a copy
of *Pickwick*. He'd read aloud for hours that night, so long that
his throat was raw for a couple of days afterward. But he
remembered that the longer he read, and the shorter the intervals between Lucky's contractions, the more likely she was

to laugh so hard that he'd stop reading until he figured she was able to hear him again. They were also timing the intervals between contractions, and she'd held off the nurse who kept wanting to send her up to the delivery room so determinedly until she was convinced it was time, that when she did finally go up, Mark was born within minutes of her arrival—born, she told him in great exhilaration when she was brought back to the room an hour or so later, just as the first rays of the rising sun broke through the delivery room windows.

His fatigue must have become decisive though finally as he recalled this, for the next thing he was aware of was Faith's voice, faint but unmistakable, saying, "You know, old friend, maybe you ought to go to bed."

She was lying just as she'd been lying when he'd looked at her last, but her eyes were open now, and he was sure she'd been watching him for a while before she spoke. "That's an improvement," he said.

Her face hardly changed expression, except that her eyes tightened quizzically a bit before she said, "How long have I been staging this dress rehearsal?"

He considered a moment, and decided it must be close to morning when he heard the shower running in their bathroom which backed up to Faith's bathroom. "Not as long as you might think," he said. "About two days—or a little more."

As he waited then for her to accommodate this information, the doorbell rang in their apartment, and then there were footsteps going down the hall. The footsteps were Lucky's, so it had to be Sarah who was in the shower. Then the hall door opened, and Lucky said somewhat enigmatically, "Oh, you're back."

"In something less than triumph," Carl answered.

13

NOTHING THAT HAPPENED in the next several days met the expectations of renewal roused by those simultaneous returns —of Carl from Guatemala and Faith from somewhere less locatable. He observed as usual, and he listened to statements some of which were spontaneous and some answers to questions he'd asked, but he could have little extended exchange with anyone, since anyone to whom he looked for this was more or less invalid. Carl, who was suffering the consequences of a bad bout of dysentery, was effectively out of circulation, and though Faith had come back from the edge, she'd come no more than partway back. In the middle of the day, with Annie's help, she shifted once more now from her bed to her chair, but she stayed up only a couple of hours, and tended even then to be distant and preoccupied and to flag quickly in conversation. And Sarah meanwhile was green and withdrawn.

But it was Lucky's continuing distraction that disappointed him most. At first, he attributed this to the strain she'd been under to maintain her confidence—on which he and Sarah had in turn depended—that they could do whatever needed to be done for Faith and that she probably wasn't going to die quite yet anyway. He thought he was witnessing fatigue exacerbated by disappointment at the limitations of Faith's recovery. That explanation failed to make sufficient continuing sense though when he heard her on the phone with Phil or Mark confirming plans for Faith's now rapidly appproaching birthday, or discussing these plans with Faith herself. He then had to conclude that she must not really have expected her mother to make much more of a recovery than she had, and he also assumed that after having managed one crisis so well, she was more confident than she could have been before of being able to manage whatever was still ahead.

Faith's state of mind though too must have been complex, for her interest in what Lucky told her was unembarrassed, detailed, and somewhat ironic. "I'm very glad not to have caused this party to have to be cancelled," she said once, and amusement hatched her all but fleshless face with fine lines that had no depth.

"So are we all, Mother," Lucky told her. "It should be a splendid occasion."

He could hear neither irony nor anxiety in Lucky's response, only satisfaction. But something was also muting her satisfaction, and if that wasn't concern about her mother, he had to suspect that the ecology of concern left place now instead for postponed but accumulated concern about Sarah.

He didn't talk with Lucky about what had taken place when he ultimately got to see Peter Drew in Massingham until the evening after Carl's return. She'd expressed no desire to know about this previously, and he'd deferred to her priorities and to the obvious order of urgency and volunteered nothing. But her interest when she did finally ask about it wasn't perfunctory, and neither was her disappointment when he told her how Drew had countered his request. "I never thought it was better than a very long shot that you could work anything out without Carl," she said. "And when you come right down to it, that card's been around long enough to have done any damage it's likely to do already. It probably doesn't really matter whether something gets worked out now that Carl's back either."

Unillusioned common sense once more, but he saw her face sag as she delivered herself of it, and thought he was witnessing the particular resolution of discouragement effected by loss of the hope that holds out against good sense. She'd also had a long phone conversation by then though with Sarah in which they talked about what Sarah had talked to him about a couple of nights previously at Faith's bedside, and she was visibly and audibly upset when she told him that the conversation had taken place. "I gather this is all known to you already," she said, "and I can understand why you didn't choose to tell me about it. Why you preferred to let Sarah tell me herself. It's her distinctive problem, and I wouldn't want to try to explain it either. However much on different tracks I've always known and said the two of them were, I never expected anything quite as confused as this. Between them, each pulling stubbornly a different way, they can create perfect confusion. They're now talking about whether to get married, but Sarah declined to tell me how those deliberations were going. It was too complicated to summarize, she said, which is a way to make a virtue of confusion. Complication isn't always something to cherish. There's much to be said for retaining some capacity for simplicity. They've been together for more than two years, and whatever their ups and downs they do seem to like each other. And if she's been trying to get pregnant and Carl's done nothing to keep that from happening, that may not be an understanding exactly, but it approaches one. Why can't they take their chances and get married then like other ordinary people? What's so special about their complications? Everybody has complications, but not everybody treasures them as achievements. I'd give my eye teeth to know what they are saying to each other."

He hadn't had much to offer in response to this uncharacteristically lengthy complaint. His need to know what Sarah
and Carl were saying to each other was fully as urgent as
Lucky's, but it was also significantly different. Unlike her,
he'd been hoping more often than not for some time that they
would eventually get married, and her hope until recently that
they wouldn't had to have something to do now with her
exasperation. But he was also finding her exasperation con-
tagious. He'd been dismayed to have Carl volunteer nothing
at all about marriage in the course of their brief meeting in
Somerville, though he was very forthcoming about the matters
Ben had come to ask him about. He was both grateful and, in
one particular, surprised to hear about the initiatives taken on
his behalf while he was away. He'd known Ben was on his
side, he said, but been less certain about Lisa who had every
reason to let him stew in his own juice, particularly in regard
to anything having to do with the Miller Labs affair. He very
much appreciated the interest each of them had shown in his
welfare. The situation however had arrived at what looked to
him like an impasse. He certainly wasn't going to interfere
with Peter Drew's odd but admirable enterprise, and it should
he thought be obvious that he couldn't offer Marvin the reassurance he'd asked for.

He'd said little more than that, responding to whatever was
asked or told him so promptly that his replies felt almost rude.
He did however apologize for his brevity. He was too fagged
out still to discuss anything at length he said, but he promised
to call Ben in a few days when he was feeling better so that
they could then have the real talk he knew he owed him.

Probably Carl's claim not to be up to real talk had been
justified. Scarcely the picture of health even at his best, he'd
lost enough weight in the past couple of weeks to be haggard
now. But Ben also thought he'd never before seen him look
quite so little on his own ground in the apartment in Somer-

ville. The apartment had been Sarah's for some time before they began to live together, and the discreet way he slipped into it, the relative absence of change in its appearance caused by his presence, had added significantly to the tentative air of their relationship. It simply remained Sarah's apartment. In the earlier time Ben had known him, Carl had always lived in a state of clutter that could become squalid when he was having a bad time, but that was generally salubrious enough, a working ambience in the midst of which he maintained his own carefully created personal style. Sarah however embraced an aesthetic of positive scarcity, and the few pieces of solid furniture in these four large square white rooms, the second floor of a typical Somerville three-decker, left them all but empty. Ben generally found this attractive, but today, with only Carl here, it felt unexpectedly harsh and inhospitable. While they talked, Carl half-sat, half-reclined against an accumulation of pillows of different sizes at one end of the living-room couch. Books and papers spilled out from his lap over the free surface of the couch next to him, and toast ends and the residue of a bowl of soup were on a tray on the coffee table in front of him. But this island of explicable mess was a contained intrusion into the otherwise severe orderliness of the rest of the room.

The setting of their next, longer talk then three days later was very different. Carl had remembered his promise, but said too when he phoned to arrange their meeting that he'd just received an interesting communication that he wanted Ben to see. He suggested they get together at his office in the South End. Ben hadn't been there in a long time and might have trouble finding it, he said, but they could meet at the library and walk over together. He knew Ben was spending some time at the library now anyway, and he had some library business to attend to himself.

They'd agreed, Ben thought, to meet in the lobby, but when he didn't see Carl there at the appointed time he climbed the stairs in the high hall to the upper reading galleries where he didn't find him either. Puzzled, he came downstairs again and looked into the circulation room, and at once spotted the unmistakable long back of Carl's blue coat. Made of a kind of wool velour that had been called chinchilla when Ben was a child and that he hadn't seen much since, the coat had a shawl collar that rose to mid-cranium and a flared skirt that fell to mid-calf. It might have been designed for some flamboyant if not necessarily efficient Balkan army, but Carl had picked it up some time back for five dollars at a thrift shop, and retired his old coyote-collared parka. It was a particularly expressive garment, and Ben gauged the nature of the conversation in which he was engaged now by the way his hands, pushed deep into its slash pockets, flapped the front panels of the coat abruptly to either side of him. He was standing at the circulation desk across from a heavy-set older man in rust-colored Harris tweed whose massive head, capped by an inch-long stand of steely hair, was thrust contentiously most of the way across the desk toward him. The man was talking steadily and emphatically but without hurry, his face impassive, making some point so thoroughly that his thick-lipped mouth continued to open and close with undiminished emphasis for a time after Carl had already turned and walked away.

He was looking down at the floor as he walked, his face glazed with an ambiguous smile, so engaged still in the exchange he was walking away from that Ben had to put a hand on his shoulder to get his attention. Even when he looked up then, it took him an instant to focus. "Sorry," he said. "I think I was still completing a conversation."

"With Bulldog Drummond back there?" Ben asked.

"Oh, you saw that? I'd just returned a book that was a couple of weeks overdue, and he was giving me a heavy lecture about it. Paying my fine without protest wasn't good enough. They'd sent me two notices while I was away to which I hadn't responded, but the reason I hadn't didn't interest him."

His judgments on what he took to be stupid authority were as decided still as they'd been when Ben had first known him, but they were a lot less nervous. "You don't mind meeting me here, do you?" he said. "It's not an inconvenience?"

"Not a bit," Ben said. "I have a lot of free time these days anyway."

"You and me both," Carl said. "How does it feel? Like too much of a good thing?"

"Sometimes."

"You bet."

Carl had obviously recovered energy in the past few days, and they left the library briskly and crossed Copley Square, then turned right and crossed the tracks to Columbus Avenue where they turned right again. It was about ten years since Ben had last been to the apartment on Bayard Park, and as Carl had anticipated, he was pretty much lost now on Columbus Avenue. More buildings had come down and not been replaced, and there was nothing to recognize in the extensive brick-strewn gaps this left. But he did remember the distinctive brownstone crescent when they reached the long narrow park, and remembered too that the apartment was in the basement of the third house in from Columbus Avenue. Half a floor below street level, its front windows faced on a narrow areaway that admitted daylight and even, for a brief period each day, some direct sunlight. They went through a gate in the wrought iron fence that separated the sidewalk from the areaway to which they descended by a half flight of narrow metal stairs. The door was at the far end of the areaway from the stairs, under another, broader half-flight of stone stairs that led from the street to the first floor.

Conversation had been only intermittent and casual on the
way over here, effectively in abeyance, but once they'd entered
the studio apartment from the dark entrance hall, taken off
their coats, and thrown them on the platform bed covered with
a black and white serape, this constraint came quickly to an
end. A desk, a desk chair, and an armchair, each battered but
otherwise disparate, crowded the front portion of the small
room behind the barred window onto the areaway, and after
motioning Ben to the armchair, Carl brought the desk chair
out from behind the desk for himself. He didn't sit down
though, but began to talk instead on his feet. "I want to make
sure I have this right," he said, "since I was pretty dim still
when we talked the other day. Marvin really did tell you he
thought I was making too much of my participation in a few
anti-Vietnam demonstrations, the fact that I smoked a lot
of pot and tripped occasionally, and my couple of years in
Canada. And the basis for this judgment was that our enlight-
ened or at least pragmatic government simply didn't disqualify
anyone any longer on such common grounds. The proof of
this being that if they did, he couldn't possibly have been
where he was today himself."

"That was about it," Ben said.

"Only he ultimately added I gather that I could be in trouble
if by any unlikely chance I'd done something 'humongously
stupid' that he just didn't know about. Don't I have that right
too, 'humongously stupid'?"

"You have it right," Ben said.

"He really is a mealy-mouthed crook!" Carl said.

His face turned unexpectedly thoughtful now, and he sur-
veyed the small room attentively as though to see its congested
disarray as Ben was seeing it. The character of the room was
undecided, neither quite residence nor quite office. Most of
the surface of the bed was covered with books and papers, but
an irregular margin was left clear on the near side with a couple

of pillows one on top of the other at the head where it was still possible to lie down. A glass coffee maker on a hot plate on the bureau was coated with dark stains. A couple of coffee cups, also stained, shared a piece of otherwise open floor with some newspaper clippings for which one cup was acting as a paperweight. "The thing is," Carl said, "that I'm sure Marvin's always suspected even if he couldn't be certain of it, that I had a hand in the Miller Labs fire, and he'd certainly call that a 'humongously stupid' piece of work. I had the chief hand in fact, the planning hand, in setting the fire, and though so far at least neither he nor the F.B.I. can apparently prove that I did, if they're really going over my history with a fine tooth comb the facts are likely to comb out. All they'd really have to do is ask me about it, and I'd tell them. How much do you know yourself though about the whole Miller Labs affair and my part in it?"

"Some, not a lot," Ben said.

"I know I never talked to you much about it," Carl said, "but I've never talked about it much to anyone. It even took me a long time to tell Sarah, only maybe that was different. What inhibited me particularly from talking much to her about it I guess was that Lisa has so much to do with the story."

He paused, intentionally, and then said, "If I talk about Lisa will that make you uncomfortable?"

"I doubt it," Ben said.

"I didn't think so," he said. "You obviously remember that she and I were living together when I first met you, but that we weren't getting on very well. Or not consistently anyway. And you've probably gathered too that one of the several disturbances between us was her low respect for my political activities."

When Carl laughed now, he also lifted his head in an abrupt motion that displayed the miniature beard under his chin.

Scarcely more than an amplified tuft, it was as pale as his skin, and its position, its size, and this virtual absence of color made it inconspicuous most of the time. "I have to believe that wasn't the fundamental trouble between us," he continued, "since I no longer set a much higher objective value on those activities than Lisa did then. At the time though, her attitude was very hard to take. Not just that it wasn't supportive. It also reflected a lot tighter view of human possibility than I could accept. And she was living by that view as well as airing it. She earned part of her college expenses by working several nights a week as an attendant at a residential school for disturbed kids. School so to speak. It was a vast juvenile booby hatch, and working there was a perpetual trial. Things never got better and they frequently got worse. But that was also what made it Lisa's idea of genuine work, and of genuine politics. My stuff was too airy for her, and she was always telling me that if I could just bring myself to think smaller I'd find some more concrete and more satisfying things to do.

"She was particularly derisive about the guerrilla theatre activities as we so quaintly called them that were occupying a lot of my attention then, and the frustrations these activities were causing me. And when I say 'then,' I'm thinking pretty precisely of the time you and I got to know each other and the ways I and some of my friends were comporting ourselves in the service of what we also rather risibly called activism. Ways that you expressed a sympathy for incidentally that I expected and wasn't getting from Lisa, starting the very first time we met when I got run over by the cops down the block from your old house and you took me in off the street. And of course first met Sarah. Lisa thought that whole incident was hysterical, but I'm not exaggerating when I say that it and a few other incidents like it had brought me to a state of frustration that was nearly intolerable. No matter what we thought we were doing, we always seemed to end up suckering ourselves. Time after time we were just giving the cops another chance to dispose of us as kids. I guess I really found myself even then in a lot less than total disagreement with Lisa about these activities, but that didn't help our relationship either, since I couldn't admit what I thought even to myself. When the idea of doing something very different finally came to me however, I knew that though it still wasn't the kind of thing Lisa thought I should be doing, it could be said to follow logically from what she'd been telling me. Could be my way of saying, 'Okay, sure, I can think concrete, but I don't intend to think any smaller than I have to.' I'd told her frequently, using the interesting idiom of the day, that I wouldn't go in for band-aiding. You must have heard that often at the time. How we weren't going to put any more patches on the old system. That we meant to do nothing less than surgical removal."

As Carl's narrative gathered intensity, he began to move on a tight, set course. Hands on his elbows, arms pressing his non-existent belly, he'd take a couple of short steps in the direction of the platform bed, wheel, and return. This carried him off and then back onto the small rug in the center of the floor, and the alternating sounds his boot heels made on the rug and on the floor accentuated the menace of his tightly arced body. To Ben, close to and below him, he looked heedless, as though only his arms pressed around his body kept him from crashing into the furniture, the walls, even his auditor. This impression of forcible constraint was increased by the way his arms could appear to belong to someone else, as though they were wrapped around him from behind. Yet it didn't take much deliberation to realize that he was working hard to contain and order his unruly images of the time he was talking about as they asserted competing claims for priority, and that it might have been only the way his arms bound his guts that allowed his narrative to be coherent.

"A lot of our endeavor that year was concentrated on Miller Labs," he said. "They were at hand, and they could hardly have stood for more of the stuff we thought we had a responsibility to call to public attention. Miller was an independent lab, but all of its contracts came from the Defense Department and most of its research was directed by scientists from M.I.T. or Harvard. And we'd learned or been told—a distinction we didn't pursue very rigorously—that they were working on heat-directed missiles. Smart missiles that would search out a 98.6-degree target and nothing else. Bad stuff! Even if our information was only half accurate, I still don't think it was stupid to pick them as a representative enemy. They were— and they still are moreover. What was stupid though was to think we were going to do anything significant about them. And part of the time we really did persuade ourselves that we were mounting a growing campaign that was ultimately going to close Miller down. We even talked sometimes about making it happen sooner by direct assault."

Carl had transported himself back into the events he was talking about, and as much was being said by the responses that played across his pale registering face as by what was actually spoken. Even his pauses for reflection were expressive. "We'd scheduled demonstrations at Miller that fall and winter," he said, "on the second Thursday of every month, and after the first couple of months everyone had learned their parts—we, the cops, the people at Miller. Their suppliers knew not to schedule deliveries on the days we were coming, and the employees brought their lunches with them and holed up until we were gone. The cops would put up their barriers first thing in the morning, prescribing the areas where we could and couldn't demonstrate. Demonstrate! That doesn't take much thinking about either. But anyway, we'd arrive a little after noon in our affinity groups, and bunch together on our side of the barriers. Then, one after the other, the designated speakers of the day would take the bull horn and tell us how what Miller was doing was evil, and how though Ho Chi Minh was going to win anyway, we meant to make it easier and faster for him to do that. It was a way of course of talking to ourselves collectively—or of dreaming aloud. For all the response we got from those impassive ugly buildings, the lab could have been closed already, but we knew it wasn't. And the tactical police across the barriers from us were remarkably unresponsive too. They never appeared to hear these speeches. Not even when, as happened sometimes despite the current wisdom against it, one of the speakers talked about the pigs. At the second demonstration however, one cop found some way to make his attack dog howl whenever a speaker made a more than ordinarily grandiloquent threat or promise. Then, as soon as that one dog began to howl, the others would take it up, creating a chorus that was both intimidating and thought-provoking.

"It's hard to keep up your enthusiasm for that kind of a routine, and after the November demonstration, we knew we'd have to step things up or call it quits. There'd been an appreciably smaller turn-out in November than in October, and as the weather got still colder it was going to be even harder to get people to turn out. But if attendance fell much more, we could be treated as a simple nuisance. The cops could pick us up on trespass charges or just run us off. The only step-up we could manage to agree on for December however was to allow but not call for acts of disobedience. And individual, not collective acts. Anyone so inclined was to feel free to duck under the barriers and get arrested."

Carl stopped pacing now, the long skinny bow of his body

lost tension, and he folded onto the desk chair. "Have you ever been arrested?" he asked. "Whether because you wished to be or otherwise?"

Ben told him that on one occasion he'd thought about getting arrested for cause and decided against it, probably because he was chicken, but Carl wouldn't accept that explanation. "Not at all," he said. "You were just intelligent enough to know that it would be a humiliation whether you gave yourself over or they took you over. I experienced it twice, once each way, early on in my limited career as an activist, and both experiences were bad. I knew right off this time therefore that I wasn't going to invite the cops to humiliate me again. Not at least for nothing. I had a different and more palatable idea.

"The November demonstration took place only a few weeks after you saw me playing that tight game with the cops on the street in front of your house, and the limits of possibility of that occasion must still have been nagging me as I stood out in front of Miller Labs for the third time doing nothing and trying to pretend to myself that it was something. Not much, but at least something. And right in the middle of one of the more preposterous speeches I'd ever heard made by a supposed friend, punctuated by the responses of the dogs that seemed so appropriate I could almost imagine that I was howling with them, my eye fell on that shack with the sign Miller Laboratories Building #4 over it the way the eye of a man dying of thirst would fall on a spring or watering hole. Or of course on a mirage."

Carl was looking directly at Ben now, and the quick play of light in his eyes, bright flecks that never stayed in the same location for more than an instant, suggested a confusing fluctuation between immediate involvement and distancing amusement. "Building #4 was an inflated title for what was really there," he said. "Miller was raking our money in hand over fist, and they kept all their real estate spruced up to help make the point that no matter what was said about them, no one could say they weren't responsible neighbors. However cosmeticized the building was though, I was sure that it was only a place to park bicycles under cover, or to stow lawn mowers or snow blowers or other non-critical equipment. I found out later that what was actually stored there was soap and other cleaning materials, paper towels, and toilet paper— a hell of a lot of toilet paper—but that one end of the building unfortunately was also a lounge for janitorial personnel. A place for them to eat their lunches and have a hot and cold drink machine. I suppose they didn't feel absolutely at home with the Ph.D. crowd in the neighboring bistros. It never for a moment occurred to me though that the building could have been used for anything like that, and it caused me considerable shame and pain when I discovered that with sure political instinct we'd struck a blow against Miller's least privileged class. But all I really saw when I first focused on the building, just when the howling of the dogs suggested to me that my own voice had undergone some dreadful transformation, was that it was clearly and identifiably enemy property, but that its comparative isolation from the rest of the establishment made it vulnerable. I assumed too, as I said, that it was of too little consequence for Miller to worry about it very much. But what signified for my need was that it was on our side of the barriers, that there were no cops anywhere near it now during the demonstration, and that it was plainly identified as enemy property by the long sign across its facade. Then—and this really did it—I remembered I'd also looked across at this build-ing frequently from the windows of an apartment that had belonged to the girl I'd been going with before Lisa. Another chapter of my bad past. Moreover, the apartment had changed hands, and one of the guys who lived in it now was actually in my affinity group. You can see how it all must have seemed providential."

Ben said he could understand how it might have seemed so, but doubted that he would himself have taken even that concatenation of circumstances as a convincing summons to arson. He also realized though, he added, that this might indicate mostly his own socialized limitations.

Carl looked mildly surprised first, and then amused. "You sound just like my father," he said. "It's not the only time you have, but I didn't expect it this time. I've thought about that generational difference a lot. Partly it must have to do with something I know we've talked about before—the opportunity you and he both had at the age I was then, and that I didn't have, to do something large, risking, and presumably significant. Action for the common good. I find it more than a little embarrassing to have to put it that way, but I think it's accurate nonetheless. Vietnam just didn't provide me with anything much like the opportunity that the Second World War provided for both of you."

"I remember, we have talked about it," Ben said, but didn't say how well he'd remembered these conversations recently or why.

"My father would hate to think that he'd had any direct or even indirect fostering influence on this plan," Carl said, "but it was on his bookshelves the previous summer that I discovered a book called *New Ways of War* by a guy named Tom Wintringham who'd commanded the British Battalion of the International Brigade in Spain. I'd have been inclined to think it found its way onto his shelves by mistake if I hadn't found his name and the date 1941 written on the flyleaf. I couldn't have imagined my father ever buying a book like that before I found it, but now I had to try at least to imagine it. A salutary effort even if it didn't get me very far.

"The book itself though didn't get me very far either. As a handbook, it offered little that was useful for what we were up to in Cambridge, Massachusetts, in 1970. But the ring of its ideology made my blood beat in my ears. I can still recite one of the book's many injunctions word for word. 'To-day it is the duty of all citizens of a democracy to understand this business of fighting for a People's War is the only effective answer to Totalitarian War.' Did my father's heart ever rise to this lousy prose in anything like the way my heart rose to it again just in recollection as I stood in front of Miller Labs and contemplated the unexpected opportunity afforded me by Building #4? I have no way of knowing. I've never said anything to him either about setting the building on fire or of course about the determining influence of this book I swiped from his library on my decision to do it. I'm not sure why. I wonder why I haven't talked to him, if it comes to that, about quite a number of things I've talked to you about at one time or another. Why that is I haven't gotten my paternity straightened out. Do you think I should try to?"

This might have been only a rhetorical question, but Ben said anyway that he didn't know Carl's father very well and had no advice to offer. He was again being reserved, for he could picture the place on his own bookshelves where his copy of the Wintringham book, which he too must have bought in about 1941, should have been. He hadn't noticed it there recently, but that didn't mean it no longer was. The orange and white spines of his old Penguins were so faded by now, that it was easy to overlook them. All he could remember clearly of the book itself though was a picture of the author, a very fit middle-aged man with a bald crown, trim mustache and side hair, and black wire spectacles—a donnish warrior in a collar, tie, and dark suit whose appearance, though a bit comic, was also appropriate to the earnest social bravado the book still

summoned to his mind even if he couldn't any longer remember any of the procedures he assumed it must have outlined
for concocting Molotov cocktails or rigging decapitating wires.

"It came to me you really might say in a flash," Carl said,
"that we should set Building #4 on fire at our next Miller
demonstration. We could take pictures of it then in flames with
the sign across it making any other identification unnecessary
and send the pictures to the newspapers. It seemed not only
a right, but a truly beautiful idea. And you can't imagine the
exquisite relief it brought me just when I badly needed some
kind of balm. The idea was too instantly commanding to be
subject to second thoughts. The question that is was never
whether we should do it, not at least until we actually had. It
was only how."

Carl was once more pacing, but his motion was more relaxed
than it had been. His arms were no longer wrapped across his
concave belly, and he gestured fluently and more or less continuously with his right hand, articulating the fingers from a
rotating wrist into a range of precise postures that had to be
intentional even though the intentions weren't quite lucid. His
voice however wasn't at all relaxed. Suppressed excitement
kept threatening to make it break.

"It turned out to be dizzyingly easy to bring this inspired
thought to fruition," he said. "And if fruition isn't the appropriate term for an act of destruction even if the destruction
was pitifully limited, in this case it really doesn't matter since
you do know what I mean. Thought became matter—though
that isn't quite right either—without any of the resistance from
the world it was to affect that I not only expected but must
in some way have counted on. I don't even like to think what
a few really imaginative kids with a taste for large effects could
do if they set their minds to it. That we did so little is evidence
more of the limits of our sense of the possible than it is of the

resistance of the actual. On the other hand, what we did do also made far less difference to the world than I could have imagined. I swear I really believed that if we managed to set Building #4 on fire in some emblematic way, that was going to help to end the war in Vietnam and I'd then both feel and actually be an effective person. Someone whose life combined thought and action to alter its circumstances. I'd be the André Malraux of my generation."

The clang of recognition and the clang of non-recognition sounded simultaneously now for Ben in a rattling mix. Though he'd had strikingly similar illusions at times about the significance of what he was doing in the course of what Carl thought of as his comparable but larger opportunity, he'd had no even vaguely similar notions about what he was making of his life, maybe just because the opportunity was ready-made and didn't have to be invented. But Carl didn't give him much time to think about this. "However silly the illusions that formed the aura of this act for me though," he was saying, "I believe even now that I contrived the doing of it with the sure instincts of a born terrorist. There was to be no guerrilla theatre this time. This was to be the real thing, and it was to be a communal act. But I also knew that unless we kept the participating community small, something was bound to go wrong. Surprise was essential, and surprise required secrecy. The job was to be done therefore by my affinity group without even consultation with anyone else. Two men and three women on the ground, and one man with a camera at the second floor apartment window across the street to place us in history. And, remarkably, the six of us agreed on a plan and then managed to keep our mouths shut for the three weeks between the time we decided what we were going to do and the time we did it. And when the time came, we did just what we'd decided to do like veterans, even though as you know I was in such a

terrible funk for several days just before we did it that I almost
called it off. Or thought a lot about calling it off anyway. I
was sure we weren't up to it. Sure particularly that I wasn't.
It was because I was already in such a terrible state that Lisa
moved out for a while, not the other way round. That was
one of the several times we split on a trial basis before we split
for good. I've never been in that deep a hole again, and I hope
I never will be. And though I climbed out of it finally, and in
time, I don't think I could have done it without that big boost
I got from you."

"Even though I didn't know what I was boosting you to or
for or why you needed a boost?" Ben said. "I'd have responded
differently if I had."

"That never occurred to me. I was sure you understood all
you had to understand. Sure that out of affection and some
kind of natural empathy, you'd divined at least the general
nature of what was bugging me, which made it easy for me
to keep my pledge to the other members of my affinity group
—Tonto was our code name for ourselves, can you imagine
that?—not to say a comprehensible word to anyone outside
the group about what we were up to. You told me exactly
what I needed to hear right then from someone I trusted who
could talk from experience. And having heard you, I came out
of my funk in time, and everything went off as though we'd
been doing such things for years.

"The Thursday in December just before Christmas when
the next Miller demonstration took place was cold, clear, and
windy. The turnout was predictably modest, and when the
first few people did their acts of civil disobedience, ducking
under the barriers and sitting down on the other side, the cops
didn't even bother to arrest them. They just picked up each
one spread-eagled—one cop on each side holding an arm and
a leg, and with no sex bias whatsoever—and tossed him or

her as the case might be right back over the barrier. Over, not under. I had sympathetic spasms in my kidneys each time a back landed with an audible crunch on the frozen macadam. A lot of other demonstrators must have had similar responses, which made this simple tactic a very effective discouragement. The coldness of the day could have made a relatively warm paddy wagon seem attractive and actually encouraged more people to cross the barriers, but no one was going to imagine anything at all comfortable about slapping that icy surface back first hoping desperately you weren't going to hit your head as well. The demonstration would have been just another desultory defeat therefore if Tonto hadn't saved the day at the very end. It had been so desultory until then that we found it pretty nerve-wracking to hold our act for the end as planned.

"But we did stay on schedule, waiting until about a quarter to two to start drifting through the assembled bodies toward Building #4. Given the smallness of the assembly, drifting wasn't difficult. Then a couple of minutes before the hour, when I could see that each of the six of us including our photographer was where he or she had engaged to be, I lit a cigarette. This was the signal for the other man on the ground to light one too, and for the three women, each of whom was carrying a thermos, to empty their thermoses casually along the ground immediately in front of the building. They weren't dumping coffee though. They were dumping gasoline, and when they'd done this—which didn't take long enough to attract attention—the other man and I flipped our cigarettes into a couple of the puddles and that was that. Miller Laboratories Building #4 was instantly sealed off by a wall of flame into which the thermoses were thrown to make them unidentifiable and the five of us who'd accomplished this so easily were drifting our separate ways off again with the rest of the demonstrators who were putting distance between themselves and the flames too in some kind of astonishment. But for quite a while then anyway I wasn't feeling at all as I'd expected to feel. Instead of being elated, I was once more terrified.

"I hadn't anticipated first of all how fast that line of gasoline would ignite. It was more like an explosion than like something catching fire, an immediate transformation of the elements. We could easily have hurt some of our friends, killed someone even. It was a while before I knew for sure that we hadn't, because of the confused muddling around close to the building as people tried to disperse. While that was going on too, one of the garage doors opened, and a couple of men came bursting out through the wall of flame. I don't know how or when they'd gone in there, but there they were. Both were black, they were apparently uninjured, and once they were out the younger one sprinted across the open area and vaulted the police barrier, heading for a two-wheeled cart that carried fire-fighting equipment. The older one meanwhile stood just clear of the flames giving anyone who could hear his not very large voice a piece of his mind. He was quite old, and one of his legs was shorter than the other, and as he shifted from foot to foot in what I took to be uncontainable contempt, he was also thrusting up and down like a piston. It was pretty awful. As I say, his voice wasn't very large, and soon there were sirens sounding too and dogs barking and everyone in sight was noisily on the move, but I was in range of his voice long enough to hear him say that we were a bunch of crazy rich kids who needed to have our asses whipped. He wasn't volunteering to do that however. He sounded as though he was about to burst into tears. That's what made it so truly terrible. I was feeling thoroughly ashamed as well as scared."

Ben said he remembered reading about the fire the next morning in the *Globe*, and seeing the picture, but that it hadn't even occurred to him that Carl might have had anything to with it.

"Really?" Carl said. "Didn't you even wonder whether this

was what I'd been talking to you about, however indirectly, a few days before?"

"I don't think so," Ben said. "I didn't make the connection until you made it for me, and it must have been a couple of weeks anyway before you did that. Why didn't you say something to me sooner incidentally? Were you too unhappy about what had happened?"

"Not once I saw our photographer's pictures in all the papers the next morning," Carl said, "and knew by then too that no one had been injured and that the fire had actually been extinguished with Miller's own equipment before the city fire department had even had time to arrive. When the *Globe* ran that picture on the front page, I felt all the elation I'd expected to feel but hadn't when we did it. The picture was what I'd wanted all along, wanted a lot more certainly than I'd wanted the fire itself. The only war I really had the stomach for obviously was the war for men's hearts and minds. I was the one who did the artful lettering then under the picture on the postcard, not on the prints we sent the newspapers but on another print I kept for myself. The messianic promise. Next Year in Jerusalem. I sent copies of the picture with that message on it to the five other members of my affinity group as a New Year's card, and gave a copy to Lisa too just before we split for good. Part of my elation had come out as totally unrealistic contempt for the arms of the law. Having accomplished exactly what we'd hoped to accomplish so easily and efficiently, and without cost—with no, you might say, side effects—I figured we were immune to retribution. For a while that is I did. It wasn't until a few years later, when I'd had plenty of time to descend from that high, that I made cautious inquiries about the whereabouts of the five cards I'd sent and found out with a mixture of relief and chagrin that all of them had been destroyed. The one I couldn't find out about was the one I'd given to Lisa. Our final bust-up had taken place in a pretty messy way. I'm not sure there are any other ways, but if there are I've never experienced them. But at any event, I couldn't imagine asking her to return or destroy her copy of the card. One of the things she'd charged me with when we were splitting was losing my old convictions. That was what happened she said to people who could only think big. She didn't bother to say that she, on the contrary, was still keeping the faith, but she didn't have to. I knew well enough that in her own fashion, she was. She'd gone to work full time after graduation in the same pediatric loony bin in which she'd worked part time while she was in college, and she was now also trying to organize the place. Bring in a union. I didn't know what had happened to her copy of the card, but it certainly occurred to me that it might well be the surviving exception. That she could have mislaid it by now, but that she most likely wouldn't have destroyed it out of caution. Lisa's hard-headed, but she's not cautious. It didn't occur to me however that she might have given it away."

"But you don't sound as though you feel betrayed that she did."

"Inconvenienced maybe, but certainly not betrayed. She gave the card after all to someone to whom it meant more than it seems to have continued to mean to my fellow participants in the event."

They were beginning to have something more like a conversation now, and Carl had completed his recitation and lowered himself onto the desk chair once more. The way his feet were planted on the floor under him however suggested that he still hadn't really settled, that he'd only poised instead at a level at which he could look more directly into Ben's face. His eyes were narrowed, to limit their field, and his head was thrust back just enough to expose that soft tuft of beard that suggested an expectant sensor. If he was concerned about how fully he'd been understood however, Ben thought, he needn't have been. He understood only too inconveniently well what Carl had told him fully now for the first time. Even the fact that he could not himself, whatever the circumstances, have been a party to the setting of the Miller Labs fire had lost importance, since it was obvious to him that the present Carl could not have been a party to it either. Carl was no longer capable of the kind of conviction that had attached him so avidly to that action at the time. Nonetheless however, he could no more alienate himself from that conviction he'd once possessed than Ben could alienate himself now from the conviction that had sustained his blind roaming of the German countryside near the Elbe with some radio vehicles and a couple of half-tracks in the spring of 1945—the preposterous belief that if he failed to accomplish what he'd been sent out to do the Allied advance might be appreciably hindered. This increment of understanding had jarred uncomfortably but solidly into place when Carl said he'd actually believed that the action against Miller Labs could shorten the war in Vietnam. Said it in a tone of amused wonder. It was the very unlikelihood of such convictions, unstaled by repetition, that made them impossible to deny.

Carl hadn't though, Ben still remembered, gotten him over here today just to secure this understanding. Some additional consequence was on the announced agenda, and it seemed prudent to limit any declaration of understanding until he'd found out what that was. "Okay, I can see that," he said, "but what's this further complication you want me to know about?"

"I'll show you," Carl said.

He slid the desk chair on its casters across the rug to the bed where he removed an envelope from one of the deep pockets of his coat and then slid back again. His lean sallow face had assumed a look of insistently impure pleasure that had to be in good part vindictive. "I received a communication from our friend Marvin yesterday," he said. "A letter, and an enclosure that would be called an exhibit I guess in a court of law."

Ben could entertain the possibility that this communication might be unexpectedly benign or helpful only for the time it took for the card to be drawn out of the envelope. "I'm not sure you need to see it again, but anyway here it is," Carl said, extending it to him by one corner held between his thumb and forefinger like the proverbial dead fish. "You might not expect Marvin to frequent the kinds of shops, which can't after all be so many altogether, in which this card would have a market. But once you took time to think about it, you'd see that that was exactly wrong. I won't show you the letter unless you insist on seeing it. It would do neither your digestion nor your central nervous system much good. I'll tell you the substance of it instead. There was a message for you to begin with. Marvin wanted me to tell you that he'd found the card in a bookstore in Washington that he'd begun to frequent precisely because it reminded him of the Phoenix."

"That's nice," Ben said. He glanced at the card only long enough to confirm what he knew and then, when Carl didn't offer to take it back, placed it carefully on the desk.

"The other thing he wanted me to explain to you," Carl said, "was that he was writing directly to me because, having had no answer from you to the question he'd asked when you'd come to see him, he assumed you were reluctant to be in touch with him again. And having found the card now, he thought he could account for that reluctance."

"He's no less smart than he always promised to be, is he?" Ben said.

"It's a little different though," Carl said. "He used to be a smart mouse, and now he's a smart rat."

"I didn't find him mousy even then," Ben said, "but my

view of him was also very incomplete. What was the main point of this communication though?"

"I'm getting there," Carl said. "I just wanted to set it in its proper context by delivering this minor thrust first. You're of course not his principal target. But I also have to say that he doesn't seem to hold you in very pure affection any longer either."

"I'm aware of that," Ben said. "The last time we had anything to do with each other I disappointed him. And I was in fact stupid. I'd failed to understand how varied his talents were."

"We'll have to talk about that sometime," Carl said. "But what Marvin wanted me to know was that he'd suspected at the time it happened that I had something to do with the Miller Labs fire, and thinking about that again after chancing on this card, he was suddenly dead sure why you hadn't given him the reassurance he asked for. He can't even now, he admits, prove I was implicated in the setting of the fire, but that doesn't really matter to him. The event after all, he says, the minor conflagration, was no big deal. No one was hurt, even the property damage was trivial, and naturally there were no consequences. But nonetheless if it ever came to light that I'd had something to do with this piece of foolishness—and if I had anything to do with it, he's sure I must have had a lot to do with it, since I was never a mere follower—there'd be a stink. A silly stink to be sure, but a big one nonetheless. People in the Department would be certain to ask why Marvin Traglich, who'd known me when this occurred, hadn't at least warned them of some such possibility. He therefore had to have a contingency plan. So to make sure his own ass didn't get burned with a lot worse consequences than the old Miller building, he wanted to have a letter from me in his files in which I repudiated my part in the fire. The repudiation would have to be pretty explicit too if he was to go on as he'd like to, doing nothing to prejudice my case."

Carl paused briefly, but then continued before Ben could say anything. "I find his continuing concern for me touching, don't you?"

"Did he say anything about what explicit might mean?" Ben asked.

"That's a good question," Carl said. "He made a point of not doing that. He left it all up to me. I presume I can say anything I want, provided I make it clear that I now consider the action to have been both illegal and ill-considered. And no doubt that I wished I'd had no part in it. Or, better still, that it had never occurred."

"You don't have to start with the worst possible case," Ben said. "You could try offering Marvin something less and see what happens."

"I could," Carl said, "but you know as well as I do that I'd be a sucker if I did. Let's face it. The jig's up as regards the fellowship. Marvin has more than enough clout in the Department to see to it that it is no matter what can or can't be proved, and that's what he's going to do no matter how he protests his continuing concern for me. He has, after all, lots of reasons for not liking me, and he's not going to deny himself the satisfaction of indulging his dislike. But I don't have to give him the additional satisfaction of watching me humiliate myself by dickering with him. I won't bare my faulty inconsistent soul for him in the dim hope of gaining something I've never been sure I wanted anyway. Whatever my reservations about the Miller Labs fire—you know, however foolish or stupid it looks to me now as a political act—I also remember that in a way that still matters to me, I felt better the morning that picture appeared in the *Globe* and a bunch of other papers too right across the country than I've ever felt since. Maybe better than I'm ever going to feel again, but I can't reconcile myself to that possibility. Can't settle down with it. What's the use of the greater understanding I have now of how the world works if it only tells me what I can't do? I certainly won't be happy just getting along with what that allows me. I'd like to believe I'd had some influence on the shape of my life, made some choices. You once told me that you sometimes felt like a good German. As if you were just going along with the tide even though the tide stank because you couldn't see or join any alternative possibility. Well, that's exactly the way I feel too much of the time, though I'd never probably have formulated it quite this way if you hadn't provided me with the formulation. I don't want to hold you accountable however for just those understandings you least want me to have, or want to feel accountable for. I don't really need that formulation to know that I can't very dependably continue along the way I'm now going—or the way it's suggested to me that it would be nice for me to go—if I think I'm doing it just because I don't have either the imagination to see or the guts to pursue some other way. I have to remember therefore that I wasn't always hog-tied. Having once done something I can still in some way be proud of, I don't have to dismiss the possibility anyway of doing something I'd be proud of again. I'd hope it would be something smarter this time, but that's not the crux of the matter. Keeping that sense of possibility even fleetingly alive though may work against certain other things I'd like to have or be. I'd like for example to be a reasonably good husband and father—to talk about only what's at issue right now—but I don't know whether I can be with adequate consistency as long as that other need continues to press me."

"You'll never know if you don't give it a try," Ben said, vehemently, but aware too even as he spoke of the comic desperation of this sudden release of energy into an exhortation that was, whatever the force with which it was delivered, only a piece of common wisdom.

Carl registered this charged change with obvious puzzlement. "I not only realize that," he said, "but I've actually been prepared to act on it. Hasn't Sarah told you that I thought we should get married? She's steadier though I suppose in her view of what that would mean than I am. She sees no point to our getting married she says unless that really signifies something. Unless, for example, I propose to do something about my work life that offers some promise that I'll be around more regularly than I've been in the past couple of years. Being married wouldn't mean a lot to her she says if she was going to be managing a one-parent household much of the time anyway. And on that score I've only been able to assure her that I'd give the fellowship a fair try if I had a chance to, but that I didn't think I was going to have that chance."

"That's rather minimal encouragement," Ben said.

"I know," Carl said. "And in addition, Sarah wants something beyond that kind of encouragement anyway. She wants some assurance—not just a statement of intention, but some conviction she was picking up in her bones—that getting married would do something fundamental to resolve these conflicts that make me such a poor risk. She's a very gutsy person, your daughter. Even with a child, she'd rather go along she says as we are now, as involved free agents, than as a couple pretending to be married in the way that you and Lucky are married. You know, for better and worse, in sickness and in health, and despite full awareness of other possibilities. She's right, I guess—no, I more than guess. We're not yet ready for that. I'm not. I think I'd have to make my way there. You know, earn it. And I just haven't done that."

14

CODA

IN BED AND GLAD to be there, waiting for Lucky to return from
seeing how Faith had weathered the excitements of the party,
he was disquietingly aware of Mark stirring around in the room
on the other side of the wall behind his head. The small room
that had to serve them as both a guest room and a work room
was made smaller still by the tool bench and storage cabinets
he'd built along one wall, so that when the high-rise bed was
open to accommodate two sleepers, there was just enough
space between it and the bench to allow cautious passage. Mark
was the only occupant of the room now however, and with
the second bed stored under the first that problem really didn't
exist. His audible knocking and bumping therefore suggested
that whatever it was that had been on his mind but unspoken
earlier in the day, was still there, making him at once restless
and careless.

This room was the only guest accommodation they had now
in their reduced circumstances as apartment dwellers. Phil and
Caroline and the children were staying with Sarah and Carl
in Somerville, and the family gathering as a consequence had
two centers. The Somerville contingent had come into Cambridge for a while the previous evening, but they'd stayed in
Somerville during the day today in order not to be underfoot
while preparations were being made for dinner. Mark how-

ever, who'd joined the others for lunch, had returned early—
to help, he'd said, with whatever had to be done. Probably
he'd also wanted to talk to them about something, but neither
of these intentions had worked out very well. Ben and Lucky
had prepared so many dinners together by now, that they did
what had to be done more or less instinctively, in a compan-
ionable near silence that they found congenial, but that was
also exclusive.

Mark had hovered uncertainly in the kitchen, waiting for
requests that weren't made or opportunities that didn't become
apparent. And when, finding nothing to do, he'd settle on a
chair or table edge in a tentative fashion that kept his willing-
ness to do something apparent, it was inevitably in a location
from which they'd then have to ask him to move in order to
open a drawer or cabinet or make use of the kitchen's limited
work space. This inability to take part in what they were doing
could have been no encouragement to confidence, and it seemed
likely therefore that something that hadn't been unburdened
then was by now festering.

But by now too, Lucky was the only person with whom
Ben really needed further conversation. He didn't want extended conversation with her either, only that she say a few
words that might make him feel a participant once more, not
just the observer he'd become almost exclusively in the course
of the day. Whatever his differences with her about this long-
contemplated, problematic gathering to celebrate Faith's eighty-
fifth birthday, he hadn't anticipated how removed or objective
he'd feel when the day arrived. As if his only part in the
occasion was to be a facilitator.

That hadn't happened all at once though. It had been a
growing condition ever since his meeting with Carl in the
South End a little more than two weeks before—and since the
affect of that occasion had been reinforced by a phone call

from Charlie Coleman the following morning. Charlie, as usual, hadn't called just to gossip. "I'm afraid the tide's turning pretty decisively against him," he said after the briefest of friendly preliminaries. " 'Puzzling,' my informant tells me. But though, to put it crudely, he smells shit, so far he hasn't been able to locate it and I haven't judged it useful to tell him where he might begin to look."

For clean-talking Charlie, this was an unexpectable expression of indignation, and he'd gone on then to say he was now absolutely certain nothing Ben could have done would have brought about a different outcome. Ben had just about come to this conclusion himself already, in part for reasons Charlie knew little or nothing about, but it hadn't afforded him the comfort Charlie intended it to.

Carl's extended apologia the previous day, his account of a piece of his history and its consequences, had been very persuasive. Ben came away from their meeting pretty well convinced that Carl had done and was doing what he had to do. He'd arrived at this conviction by way of reason however, not empathy. He understood more fully now than he ever quite had before that he couldn't really imagine himself into either Carl's past or his present history. But both this understanding and his related realization that he could do nothing more to secure Carl's future with Sarah were at once illuminations and deprivations.

In this past couple of weeks however, the crisis between Carl and Sarah had somehow, for the time at least, been weathered. Sarah, who was no longer having bouts of morning sickness, looked great—looked actually very much as Lucky had looked when she was pregnant. And she and Carl were once more easy together so far as he could judge when he saw or talked to them. They appeared both to be reconciled and to be moving confidently once more on their way or ways. His own experience however could give him little fore-knowledge of what that might mean.

This multiple realization was inevitably isolating, and it didn't lessen his isolation not to know better what Lucky was thinking now about Carl and Sarah. He had encouraging notions about that, but they weren't more than notions. When Lucky talked to him, it was mostly about Faith's party, which was the business of the moment. He sensed though that she was less angry, which was anticipatable enough since she always tried to make the best of things as they were if they couldn't be changed. She'd been on the phone a lot with Sarah, planning and conferring, and he'd taken it as a positive sign as well that when everyone else had assembled in the living-room before dinner this evening, she'd asked Sarah to go next door with her to get Faith and complete the gathering.

He'd been as quiet then, waiting for the three of them to return, as he was now waiting for Lucky to return alone. One way and another recently he'd been waiting for Lucky to return from somewhere. They were on one of those circles they'd been on before when he was moving one way and she another and neither of them could know for certain that it was a circle until they finally met again face to face. Quiet as he was now, he could hear and mostly identify what Mark was doing on the other side of the wall—when he sat down on the bed, when he got up, when he dropped or knocked against something. His own silence was unfair he thought. Mark, hearing nothing, couldn't know that every move he made was audible.

For a time though earlier in the evening, in the livingroom waiting for Lucky and Sarah to return with Faith, he might have been effectively invisible as well as inaudible. He'd gone into the kitchen to check the roast, and when he returned, no one of the four adults and two children paired off in the livingroom seemed for a time even to notice him. Phil and Carl had been in adjacent chairs at the far end of the room talking, Caroline on the rocking chair rocking Flora on her lap, and Mark and Sam kneeling on the floor over a model of a nuclear submarine, and his reentry had caused nothing to change.

Odd as his apparent invisibility had been though, it had also been welcome. For the past half hour or so, he hadn't been happy to be on his feet. The sensations he was experiencing in his lower back—an occasional sharp twinge and an impression that his vertebrae were no longer in secure association—were admonitory. He'd been standing almost continuously by then for several hours, and his back was asking for respite. What it really wanted was to lie prone, but that would have been too conspicuous. He'd seated himself instead on a firmly upholstered chair, wedging his spine into a corner where it was held as though in a surgical corset.

The alarm area began to ease at once, and he decided it wasn't going to do anything more drastic, clench up or let go as he'd been afraid it might. He must either have been overdoing things or doing them wrong, but the general message he took from these symptoms was that he could no longer expect all that he'd once been able to expect of his body. The message was appropriate to the occasion too. No matter how lively he and Lucky were still most of the time, only frailest Faith stood now between them and that ultimate edge that was absolutely out there even though the earth was round, and it occurred to him that his odd absence of connection with what was going on in the room close around him might be the onset of the kind of disinterestedness he'd been aware of for some time in Faith's responses to the ambient world.

But floating in relief in the conforming and supporting corner of the good chair, he reminded himself too that his relationship to the human exchange going on around him was actually causal. The six people he was observing were two sons, a daughter-in-law, a not quite son-in-law, and two grand-children, and he was at the radial center of their presence here. Two things also struck him though with a freshness that might well have been attributable to some new, disinterested power of perception. These members of his immediate and extended family were first of all remarkably easy with each other, and in a way that didn't appear to be mere tolerance. Sam had attached himself to Mark now with a prepared agenda to which Mark was attending seriously. Head to head over the snap-out plastic parts of the model submarine, assembling them for gluing, Sam had just asked Mark whether he thought he was old enough to start making balsa-wood models "from scratch" instead of pre-cut plastic models, and Mark was telling him he didn't see why not. He'd keep an eye out for some good plans for him, he said, and he'd also send him the few tools he'd need to be "in business." Patient, serious, they both seemed happy to go on working and talking this way indefinitely, and meanwhile Phil and Carl, whom he'd once thought of as po-tential antagonists, appeared happy to go on talking together indefinitely too. He couldn't hear what they were talking about, but their compatibility had to mean either that the latent an-tagonism he'd once imagined between them had been only imagined, or else that its basis, the conflict in the claims each had on him, had dissolved as these claims became less urgent.

However compatible though, Phil and Carl did look unlikely together, and this contributed to his second impression. With Lucky and Sarah who were unmistakably related to each other out of the room, the remaining assemblage was pretty disparate altogether. Even Phil and Mark scarcely looked like brothers any longer. When they were children, he'd been told repeat-edly that they both resembled him uncannily. The joke had been that he and Lucky were obviously good planners. Sarah looked like her mother and the boys looked like their father.

Well, Sarah still looked like her mother. He couldn't see himself, and couldn't know therefore whether either Phil or Mark resembled him any longer, but he could see that they didn't much resemble each other. Mark seemed to him now to be largely self-created. His face as he knelt attentively over the model with Sam bore the marks of arduous experience so decisively, that this earned face overlay his received face. Something like this was true of his thick strong body too, and though it wasn't easy to apportion cause and consequence—to know how much these physical characteristics had been determining and how much they were a consequence of a course Mark had chosen for himself—the notable fact was that no one else in memory on either side of his family had chosen to work as he had, with his hands and muscles. But this was only the most specifiable aspect of the obscurity that interposed itself between Ben and his younger son's life. He understood far less why Mark continued to be so much of a solitary, except as this too might be the consequence of an existence that was in such large part discovered or willed, so little just evolved.

Phil's existence on the other hand was entirely evolved, and had the appearance of being continuous therefore with his and Lucky's. He had to consider the possibility though that this continuity was an appearance without strong foundation. If Phil had been able to move so readily into marriage and fatherhood because his libido was invested chiefly in becoming a doctor, a time might come when those matters that had received only passing attention would assert their deferred claims.

He was more prepared to believe that his older son still looked like him than that Mark did, but Phil also looked to him now like a Californian. Even the good shape he was in was identifiable. He used a Nautilus machine, played a lot of tennis, and had a permanent tan, and he was also appreciably slimmer than he'd been before he moved west. But all of this had some look of uneasy imposition too, and the way he was dressed today, in an all-season navy blue suit, didn't suggest sporty, laid-back, informal California at all. Even Ben had considered a tweed jacket appropriate to the occasion, and Carl and Mark were both wearing sweaters and jeans.

Caroline though, who'd always lived in or around L.A., was pure California. Phil had met her soon after he'd begun his residency in L.A., and Mark, who found letter-writing easier than talking, had written a long letter home to his parents when he'd gone out to California to visit Phil, to tell them that his brother had moved into a different world. The differences, he'd written, were absolutely basic too. He'd just spent the day on a beach near Santa Monica, where he'd discovered that the bodies of Californians, or southern Californians anyway, were significantly different from the eastern bodies he'd grown up knowing about—but never of course knowing quite enough about. The bodies all around him today, he wrote, were not just better cared for and more beautiful. They were also subject to different natural laws. An amazing number of them were flawless, possessed of none of those ordinary imperfections that, in any specific instance, he'd always thought you had to learn to love. And Phil's friend Caroline, who was fantastic on a surfboard, was also fine gold from head to toe, like some James Bond beauty except that in her case there was no recourse to gold spray.

Time had changed that somewhat now. Caroline still had the lithe body of a surfer, but her gold had faded in a dozen years, and even what was visible of it today—she was wearing a long-sleeved white wool dress and gray stockings—was obviously assisted. She was carefully made-up in ways of which Ben could specify only that her hair was frosted. Flora was pure gold, which made the difference more visible by contrast,

but Sam was a genetic mix. The brooding uncertainty of his
dark face reminded Ben of Mark when he was a child and
suggested that his affinity for Mark was predetermined.

How long had he remained wedged into the chair that way,
an effectively invisible spectator? Long enough anyway for it
to have been a distinct event. And yet no more than five or
ten minutes altogether could have gone by from the time Lucky
and Sarah left to get Faith to the time they returned with her,
he hadn't yet been on the chair when they left, and a couple
of minutes before they returned Flora slid off Caroline's lap
and came across the room to join him. Even when she'd climbed
onto his lap though, put her arms around his neck, and kissed
him, his spectatorial isolation wasn't quite finished. No one of
his own children could ever have done this, not anyway with
her apparent ease and competence, and this lovable and loving
grandchild remained a somewhat alien creature to him.

She'd asked however if he thought the party was going to
begin soon and he'd said he was sure it would. Almost at once
then Lucky and Sarah returned escorting Faith, and the several
atomized social fragments—Mark and Sam kneeling on the
floor, Carl and Phil talking together, Caroline alone, and Flora
on his lap—cohered, became an occasion. Faith was wearing
a high-collared brocaded dress that mercifully concealed her
wasted body, and she'd also left her four-footed cane behind
and was walking with one arm linked to one of Lucky's and
the other to one of Sarah's. The three women, though each a
generation apart, had entered the room as a single fused entity,
the two substantial, manifestly similar flanking presences joined
by the intense but insubstantial spirit they sustained between
them. It was a planned effect of course, though Lucky's intention had not been this exactly but rather to make the tribute
to her mother as little a memorial to her debility as possible.
Most of what happened after that, until Faith told them just

before Lucky and Sarah escorted her back to her apartment again that the occasion had been at least as gratifying as she'd hoped and expected it to be, had blurred for him already, become texture rather than discrete events. What was still vivid though was Lucky's evident conviction that she'd succeeded.

After Faith's departure, everyone had pitched in to clean up, but then not hung around very long since both Phil and Mark were making early departures in the morning. By the clock now, it still wasn't very late, but even in bed his bones were telling him that it had been a long day. Or if not long exactly, freighted—and not yet unfreighted either. Waiting for something to be said when Lucky returned, something he couldn't specify but needed, his suspense was aggravated when he heard her returning footsteps in the hall.

She came into the bedroom, closed the door behind her, then stood a moment surveying him. "That's exactly where I want to be," she said. "How did you make it so fast?"

"If I hadn't," he said, "I might not have been able to make it without assistance."

"Oh, poor Ben," she said. "But don't go to sleep quite yet. I'll join you in a moment. I just had to make sure Mother was peaceful."

She changed quickly into a nightgown, and when she went into the bathroom to brush her teeth, she left the door open to allow for conversation. He said nothing however, both because he wanted her to say something first, and because his awareness of Mark in the next room made him loath to talk loud enough anyway to be heard over the rush of running water. Mark must have heard what little they'd said already though, for no further sounds were coming through the wall. Then when Lucky came out of the bathroom again and got into bed, the door to the next room creaked open. Lucky stiffened attentively next to him, a couple of heavy steps in the hall were followed by a tentative knock on their door, and he said, "Come in."

"Is it really okay?" Mark asked. "You're both still awake?"

"Yes, dear, we really are," Lucky said.

Even after this reassurance, Mark cracked the door a few inches to reconnoiter before he opened it wide enough to come through. "I wanted to talk some," he said, "and there won't be time in the morning."

He was still dressed, but his shirt was mostly unbuttoned and one of the tails was pulled out, as though he'd started to undress but been prevented from finishing by whatever it was he needed to talk about. Mark had always had trouble shifting gears or changing course before he was ready. At different times that had been either an asset or a liability. But it persisted recognizably, and the knocks, bumps, and shufflings Ben had been hearing through the wall in the past fifteen or twenty minutes probably reflected stalled but unappeasable intention. "It's okay," he said. "Sit down."

"Thanks."

Mark spoke gravely, but his courtesy was on the edge of the comic, since he was hardly aware of what he was saying. He did however, before seating himself at the foot of the bed on the side nearest the door which was Lucky's side, make sure to locate her feet and not sit on them. He'd come into their room at night this way frequently when he was small— far more often than either Sarah or Phil—but he hadn't seemed to notice then whether he was waking them or, if he did climb onto the bed, whether he was sitting on their legs or their ribs. "It was a great party," he said. "I'm very glad you had it."

"That's nice of you to say, dear," Lucky said, and sounded startlingly like her mother.

Mark hadn't come into their room just to have that exchange of courtesies though. He was rigid with anticipation, hunched at the end of the bed with his elbows on his spread knees, hands together and fingers laced. His jeans were taut around his hard, full thighs, and the hands holding one to the other between his legs were not only hard and thick too, though they could be unexpectedly adept at very fine tasks, but also somewhat deformed. He was always breaking or bashing fingers that didn't then necessarily mend straight. "A couple of things," he said. "First of all, I really needed to know before I left how worried the two of you were about Sarah."

This was what Ben had been waiting to hear Lucky tell him, but she continued to maintain a pointed silence now. "We may not have a single answer to that question," he said, stalling.

"I guess I'd like to know what you think then, Dad," Mark said. "To start."

The soft press was a moral choice rather than a style out of calculation for Mark, but it could be deceptive nonetheless. When he said he guessed something, you couldn't be sure that indicated uncertainty. "All right," Ben said. "Yes, I do worry about her sometimes. But I should also tell you that when my mind is particularly open to possibilities of catastrophe, I worry about each of you, sometimes in ways that allow me to astonish myself. I found myself wondering for a while today, for example, whether the settled look of Phil's life wasn't premature, and whether there might not be some tests ahead of him still for which he hadn't as a consequence built much muscle."

"The kind of muscle I've built a lot of."

"One of several kinds."

"I know," Mark said. "My question about Sarah is very specific though. She and Carl seem fine, but I doubt that they would have a few weeks ago. Sarah certainly didn't sound fine when I talked to her—either while you and Mom were in Mexico, or after you got back. And I don't understand what's happened since then that's made the difference. Should I consider it reassuring that they're not going to get married? Carl told me he's going to be doing some work again for the Canadian Department of Indian Affairs, putting together a history of the project he worked on for them years ago. He'll have to spend some time in northern Ontario getting the material together, but he thinks he can do a lot of the writing here. With luck, Sarah said, he might even be here when the baby's born. It was said as though it were a joke, but how is she going to feel if he isn't here when the baby's born?"

"Bad, I suppose," Ben said, and through the sensitized, private air under the bedclothes, he was aware of how purposefully Lucky continued to withhold comment.

Mark, who'd been looking down between his feet, raised his head at this abrupt, minimal answer, and the contracted surface of his face radiated uncertainty. "Their prospects aren't exactly great then," he said.

"Not necessarily," Ben said. "But I see nonetheless that they're each doing what they've chosen to do, and I have to take that as a basis for at least limited optimism. What did you hope I was going to tell you though? That I was sure everything was going to be all right?"

"Probably," Mark said. "I guess that's what I've always wanted you to tell me."

"And I've always disappointed you," Ben said.

"I'm getting better though," Mark said. "I don't cry any more. But what about you, Mom? What do you think about the situation?"

"I've been trying to achieve your father's state of balance," Lucky said. "It makes sense, and I always intend to be as sensible as I can. I'm not quite there yet though this time."

"That's fair enough," Mark said. "I get the idea."

This was only appropriately inconclusive, but his effort to gather himself now, to get up and leave, was equally inconclusive, and this arrest of intention would hold them in arrest too as long as it persisted. Not though as it had on those earlier occasions when Ben or Lucky would take him back to his room and then remain with him until he was safely asleep again, which could frequently be a couple of hours. This time they'd remain in bed together and he'd ultimately leave alone. But caught discomfort lay between them nonetheless like a cordon sanitaire.

"I had something to tell you as well as ask you," he said after a bit. "I've been seeing a lot of someone for the past few months, since the end of the summer."

"I take it you mean a woman," Lucky said.

When Mark smiled now, his nose twitched and he put a couple of fingers to his lips as if to contain a more robust response. "Oh, absolutely," he said. "She has a couple of children, a three-year-old boy and a five-year-old girl. She and her husband split up right after the boy was born."

"And you like the children too?" Lucky asked.

"A lot, fortunately," Mark said. "This may be the best way for me to acquire a family, since I feel no great need to be a biological parent."

"You sound serious," Ben said.

"I guess so," Mark said. "It wouldn't have been inappropriate for Ann to come with me to this party. But she thought it might be distracting, and I thought she might have a heavy trip."

"Running the gauntlet?" Ben said.

"Exactly," Mark said.

"Do you want to tell us any more about her?" Lucky asked.

"I don't think so," Mark said. "I know you guys are all going to like her, but I'd rather let you find that out for yourselves. We'll come for a visit in a few weeks, when nothing else is going on."

"That will be wonderful," Lucky said.

Mark nodded in assent, but he was still not quite ready to make his departure. "I've been wondering," he said, "whether it ever seems queer to you that your three biological children are so unlike each other—or you?"

"I like it that way," Lucky said. "It absolves us of too much responsibility."

"I hadn't thought of that," Mark said. "But you guys are, you know, a hard act to follow."

The sound that issued from Lucky's lips and nostrils was part derisive, but Ben heard something less voluntary too. "Be charitable, dear," she said.

"You may be hearing me wrong," Mark said. "That was envy."

"I know. That's why," Lucky said. "Is there anything else you wanted to tell or ask us though?"

"I don't think so," he said. "I will try to get back before too long with Ann. I'd like to."

"That would be very nice," Lucky said.

Ben was so intent on this exchange that Mark had gotten up, taken the few steps to the door, opened it, and then turned with his hand on the knob to look at them again before he said, "We'll count on your coming."

"You can, Dad," Mark said.

He closed the door, and they listened to him together as he moved the short distance down the hall to the next room, and—after an interval when nothing was audible and he must this time have completed undressing—got into bed. The barrier between them was gone now, and Lucky slid toward him until they were lying hip to hip. "Well, old friend," she said quietly, "I'm done in. Are we a hard act to follow though? Hardest maybe for us to follow ourselves. But I don't want to think about that any more this evening. I'm too tired."

"All right," he said.

He knew even as he said it though that he couldn't quite feel this assent. He still wanted her to say something more. But then, as her right hip bone settled harder against his left, he knew too that enviably, preternaturally, predictably, she was asleep.

A NOTE ON THE TYPE

This book was set in a digitized version of Janson. The hot-metal version of Janson was a recutting made direct from type cast from matrices long thought to have been made by the Dutchman Anton Janson, who was a practicing type founder in Leipzig during the years 1668–1687. However, it has been conclusively demonstrated that these types are actually the work of Nicholas Kis (1650–1702), a Hungarian, who most probably learned his trade from the master Dutch type founder Dirk Voskens. The type is an excellent example of the influential and sturdy Dutch types that prevailed in England up to the time William Caslon (1692–1766) developed his own incomparable designs from them.

Composed by Crane Typesetting Service, Inc.,
Barnstable, Massachusetts
Printed and bound by R. R. Donnelley & Sons,
Harrisonburg, Virginia
Designed by Harry Ford